POSSIB

SHORT STORIES

BY

HANK TUROWSKI

C/O Paradigm Press
4912 Parkview Dr.
St. Cloud, FL. 34771
paradigmpress.com
(206) 595-1907

THIS NOVEL AND ITS CONTENTS ARE CONFIDENTIAL
No part of this document may be reproduced in any form whatsoever without the expressed written consent of the author or his duly appointed representatives.

ALL RIGHTS RESERVED
COPYRIGHT 2016 By Paradigm Press

AUTHOR'S NOTE

Why would anyone write Short Stories? Is it because a writer doesn't have the imagination or patience to construct a novel? Is it because the writer's ideas are insubstantial? Is it because many readers have limited attention spans? It certainly isn't because the writer is out to be commercially successful. Short Stories just aren't economically popular. So why write them?

For me the Short Story is a comfortable middle ground. It's a place where an idea can get bones. Where a concept can either die a quiet death or become a storyline. A place where a hundred possibilities can evolve. Where campfire folklore and things that go bump in the night can become alive. In short they are fun to write and can sometimes lead an author down an unexpected path!

I am a huge fan of critique groups. I have been a member of several and have hosted my own gatherings several times. The idea of the Short Story blossomed during my attendance at one of these groups, when I tired of listening to rewrites wondered if I couldn't develop an entire story start-to-finish that could be read and critiqued in a single sitting. So I wrote a 9-page Short Story for the group titled "He Could Make Tom Brocaw Twitch". It went over well and I continued to produce stories for the group on a nearly one-a-week basis for the better part of a year. As I plunged headlong into the process I decided to challenge myself and not limit the scope of the stories to things I was comfortable with. I picked odd topics, unusual subjects, different characters - with varying degrees of success. Some were action oriented, some poignant, some humorous, some straight out of the Twilight Zone - many were satirical. It proved to be a challenging creative exercise that made me a better writer.

Eventually I had written nearly sixty stories. One of them I developed into a screen play that I sold twice to a small-time producer. I put all the stories together into the three-book sets shown below. This is the third book in the Series. They are worth the reading.

I cannot fail to acknowledge my many friends, whose quirks I sometimes borrow to immortalize in these pages, and who suffer with good nature, the odd characters who coincidentally possess their names.

I acknowledge the fantastic support of my wife Elaine, who is my partner in this process.

Finally, there's Hank Jr., the mathematician, computer scientist, and my wunderkind, who gave me ideas for some of these stories.

ISBN: 978-1537251271.

Published in 2016 by Paradigm Press, 4912 Parkview Dr. St. Cloud, FL. 34771. To order - Call (206) 595-1907 or E-Mail paradigmpress.com. *All Rights are Reserved.*

Cover Art by Helene Murré at Facebook.com/murresart

HE CAN MAKE TOM BROCAW TWITCH

"I just met a young man who claims he can make Tom Brokaw twitch."

Pouty lips parted, Susan Jeffers halted the examination of her manicure. Thirty-two, Nordic blonde, intelligent - and incredibly arrogant – Susan crossed her long legs and flashed a haughty glance my way. Every eye in the conference room watched, noting the gentle rise of her delicate eyebrows, the cascade of hair on the shoulders of her dark suit, and the subtle pressure of her breasts against her silk blouse. She took a deep breath, driving the other male attorneys into a frenzy of lust - and the females into jealous rage.

"What did you say about Tom Brocaw, Henry?" she asked. Her voice held a tinge of annoyance. But just a tinge. After all, I was the senior partner in the firm, and Susan, if her looks and luck held, had another ten years before she would reach my level.

"I met a young man, perhaps your age, Susan, who claims in complete honesty that he can make Tom Brocaw twitch – right in the middle of a newscast."

"Surely you don't believe him?"

I paused. "This morning I would have laughed at the idea. This afternoon - I'm not sure what to believe."

I turned to J. Mark Foley, our other senior partner. "Mark, if you don't mind," I said, "I'd like to relate a story." I chuckled. "It's far more important than strategic planning and case budgets."

"By all means, Henry."

Susan, boredom written in scowling lines across her forehead, started to rise. "Well, Mr. Feeney, if it's all the same to you, I have a million things to do."

"It's not all the same to me, Susan!" I replied. "Please sit and listen. It won't take long, and maybe – just maybe - you'll learn something. Like I did."

Susan, face reddening, settled into her seat. The conference room quieted.

I stood. I always did my best thinking and talking on my feet. I walked to the windows that lined an entire wall of the sumptuous room. Uptown Manhattan spread out before me, and I could see activity in Central Park two blocks away. I looked down to the street in front of the office.

I began a slow circle of the huge oak conference table as I collected my thoughts. Heads turned to follow my progress.

"Does everyone here know how to get to the Catherine Street Court House?"

Most of the attorneys looked at me as if my question was part of a college quiz and I had asked a trick question. No one seemed anxious to answer.

Susan broke the silence. "Of course we know where the Court House is, Henry. We spend most of our lives there."

I stopped behind Susan. "Ah ha! But that's not the question I asked, Susan. I grant we all know where the building is, but how many of you know how to get to there? And more importantly, have any of you ever walked?"

I noted the puzzled faces as I continued my walkabout.

"When I was younger, I walked to the Court House two or three times a week. It's a mile or two, but I was young and energetic, and the walking did me good – gave me time to think." I laughed. "Some of my best legal arguments evolved during those walks, and I'd forgotten how stimulating they used to be – until today."

Susan fidgeted.

I had completed a circuit of the room. Again at the windows, I pointed downward. "Outside the office - on the street - it's pristine, controlled, and efficient. Like the rest of you, I've gotten into the habit of calling for Charlie when I have a Court appearance. But today the weather was fine and I felt a yearning for something more than the plush seats in the back of a limo. I decided to walk."

I began another circuit. "It's a different city today than the last time I walked. Oh, there's still traffic, polite doormen, and unsmiling men and women hurrying to meetings. But that's just the facade. All the order and discipline ends when you turn the first corner. That's when you hit the grit and the chaos. And that's where I met the man who can make Tom Brocaw twitch."

I paused to look at each face. The impatience I had noted earlier had disappeared – even from Susan - and most of the audience, particularly the younger attorneys, were leaning forward and listening. I smiled. J. Mark used to say that I could "Waltz" the jury like no other attorney in the city.

"I was shocked at the changes I saw. It used to be you could count on New York's finest to roust the vagrants - maybe even drop them off in New Jersey. But now, the city teems with the hapless and the helpless."

I stopped walking. "Frankly, I resented the intrusion, but I decided to bluster through. I made myself oblivious to the curses, the smells, the awkward body motions, and the cries of anguish."

"The homeless aren't easy to ignore," I continued, "but I had a meeting at the Court House with an important judge."

I stopped again. "Any of you know where the Saint Henry's Downtown Shelter is?" Of course they didn't, and this wasn't a morality lecture, so I continued. "It's only three blocks from the Court House. I never knew it existed until today.

"The homeless congregate outside the Shelter. I had to tred gingerly not to step on them, and when I let my gaze wander, I almost tripped over something on the sidewalk. A paper bag wrapped around a wine bottle. By accident, I had kicked it. The bottle skidded across the concrete and came to rest at the feet of a handsome young man.

"At first, I thought he was a social worker. He noticed me. Shaking his head sadly, he picked up the bag and put it into a trashcan. Almost in tears, he raised his voice and shouted."

"Work is the curse of the drinking class!"

I recognized the quotation from Oscar Wilde, and I paused, trying to figure out why he had used that quotation, when I heard a sad voice behind me.

'Crazy, huh?'

I didn't want to be trapped in a discussion. Especially not there on the street. I turned slowly. I tried not to make eye contact with the speaker, but his next words grabbed me by the throat.

'He's my son.'

Shaken, all I could do was sputter.

The man continued. '*I come here every day to watch him – and listen.*'

Another shout interrupted us. **"What's the difference between man and the animals, you ask?"** I turned toward the young man, who laughed loudly before continuing. **"Why, <u>our</u> pelts have no value!"**

The father grunted, *"Absolutely crazy!"* The father was probably my age – early fifties. Yet his face was etched with tired lines, his posture deflated, and his eyes shown with an inner pain and desperation.

Another shout. **"Is the moon really revolving around the earth, or do they revolve around each other?"**

The man tried a pained, unconvincing smile before he spoke again. '*His name is Patrick. He grew up not far from here on Long Island.*'

I didn't need to be bothered like this. I nodded, muttered some trite phrase, and started to turn away. But the man spoke rapidly.

'*Patrick is twenty-five. Until ten years ago, he was as normal as you or I.*' The man paused, and I could see tears rising in his eyes. '*As a child, Patrick was tested as 'extremely gifted'. Did great in school – and in sports   Had lots of promise!*"

I told the man I was sorry and started to move off, but he brought out an old photo album he had been holding under an arm. '*Here. Just a minute, please! Let me show you something.*'

Another yell. **"They're always watching us, you know. They know where we live. The know what we eat."** The young man laughed. **"But I tricked them. I pulled out all my metal fillings. Now they can't send signals into my head."**

I stared at the father. "He didn't???"

The man smiled. '*Yes, he did. About three years ago. He got two or three out with a screwdriver before they put him away for endangerment.*"

The father spread the book on the trunk of a car and motioned me to look. I felt compelled.

'*This is Patrick when he was only a few months old. He was already sitting up and his grip was incredible.*' I looked at the photo - a smiling baby - and I couldn't resist glancing at the young man, whose speech had now turned to loud, almost incoherent rants – some, incredibly foul. It was hard to make the connection between the photo and the offensive screams - until I looked closely at the eyes. Yes! Those were the same eyes. But a wild, vacant look had replaced the innocent smile.

'My only son.' The man continued in a rush of words. 'His mom died in a car wreck when he was ten. *When he was fifteen his behavior changed. Wouldn't listen. Stopped going to school. Then he got mixed up in the wrong crowd. One night his friends dumped him on the lawn in front of the house. He was having convulsions, his breathing was ragged, and his heart was beating wildly. My God! It was horrible! I thought he was going to die in my arms. I held him until the ambulance arrived. They told me it was a drug reaction but that he going to be okay. I couldn't stop crying'.* The man looked at me through tears, but he laughed. *'I haven't stopped crying since.'*

I studied his sunken cheeks and hollow eyes. "Have you tried a hospital?" I asked. "Treatment programs?"

'Of course!" he answered. *"I worked for the City as an engineer - had good benefits. Sure! I put him in hospitals and took him to counselors. As a child, it was easy to get him medical and psychiatric help. But something inside Patrick always drew him back to the friends and off his medications.'*

"Well, I'm sorry, but…"

"There is no God but Caesar, and that salad stinks!"

'Have you ever known a crazy person?' the father asked.

His question had startled me. "No," I answered slowly, "I don't think so. Although, I've known judges whose decisions come pretty darn close to insanity."

The man ignored my joke. *'The doctors explained it to me. Severe manic depression maybe a touch of schizophrenia! Usually starts in the early teen years. No cure! Medicine can help – but only a little.'*

Before I could answer, he continued. *'For him, everything's muddled now.'*

"Listen," I said softly, "I really am sorry. I raised two sons myself. I know how difficult it is. But I have a very important meeting…"

The man laughed. *'You ever been inside a mental hospital?'*

"What?"

'Not a sanitarium' he continued,*'* but a real 'nut house'?'

7

'No,' I answered. 'I'm sure I haven't."

'It's horrible! They put Patrick there. It almost killed me!"

His eyes were pleading, tortured. I was afraid he was going to make a scene, so I stepped back, thinking I would slip away, but the man spoke quickly, his words a loud jumbled rush of emotion.

'They put my son in the 'loony bin', mister! And every time I visited, he cried for me to get him out. He said the crazy people scared him. God knows they scared me too! He swore he'd be fine.'

The man paused, then stared at the album. Something he saw made him smile. He was still smiling when he looked up at me and spoke again. *'So I made a fuss that they heard all the way to Albany. I told the politicians that my son was not some demented criminal. He was no danger to any one. He deserved to be free!'*

"**And this above all,**" the young man shouted. "**To thine own self be true. And it shall follow as the night the day – thou canst not then be false to any man!**"

At the start of the quotation, I had turned toward Patrick. He spoke Hamlet's words as if I were his only audience.

"He got that one right!" I said, but the father wasn't listening. Instead, he stared at the gutter. Once again, I thought I had my cue to escape. However, as I raised my foot, he leveled a desperate glance.

"I was wrong. Terribly wrong! I should have been careful about what I prayed for."

"What? Why?"

'Because they let him go!"

"But that's what you wanted!" I said.

"I was a fool!"

Patrick shouted. "**I can make Tom Brocaw twitch whenever I want!**"

The young man had my attention now. I turned, but the father continued, *"Patrick went back to the streets the day they let him loose."*

Laughing, the young man shouted. "**I discovered the talent by deducing that Mister Brocaw must be timid by nature – all of us great performers are.**"

"It took me weeks to find him," the father said. "Had to quit my job. Dear God, I never knew how many dirty alleys and filthy hovels there are in this City until I started searching."

"The trick, you see," Patrick continued, **"involves channeling!"**

Eyebrow raised, the young man looked at me. By his smile, I assumed that he wanted me to know he had used the play on words intentionally.

I laughed, encouraging the performance. He was a delightful rogue.

The father grabbed my sleeve. *'Sir! Please! You have to listen to me!'*

I became annoyed. I thought about calling a policeman. I stared at his hand until he released my jacket, then I returned my attention to Patrick.

Patrick continued as if nothing had happened. **"The right side of Tom Brocaw's face is slightly lower than the left side. He didn't want me to know that. That's why he tilts his head when he speaks... But I know his secret."**

"I found Patrick living in a dumpster!" the father continued. *"Eating whatever was tossed inside. There were maggots in his shoes and filth in his hair. He was afraid of me. It took an hour to convince him I was his father before I could coax him out."*

"So, what I do," Patrick yelled, **"is concentrate on that deformity and make it so big it drags the rest of his face down. He twitches to right himself. But I pull the face down again. It's a Nightly News contest only he and I know about. And it works every time. Try it yourself."**

"Patrick was hurt," the father continued. *"He couldn't sit, so I stood against that filthy dumpster and held him while he cried. He knew me then. My smell. My feel. My touch. You don't forget that stuff.*

"I left him to get food and water. Ten minutes – no more than that, I swear. When I returned, I found three men there. Evil men - with hard, soul-less eyes. I heard Patrick crying. They had shoved him out of sight behind the dumpster. One was acting as a lookout and the other two – they were doing things to Patrick.

"I guess I went nuts. The lookout tried to stop me, but I always carry pepper spray. I doused his face from ten feet away and kicked him between the legs. He screamed, and the others came at me. As they circled, I squirted them both, then pretended to reach for a gun.

They grabbed their buddy and ran. I chased them for a block, and I would have killed them had I caught them, but I'm getting too old, I guess."

I was horrified! I patted his arm, but Patrick yelled. **"What kind of shit do they feed us when we live on the streets? All the shit no one else wants to eat!"**

The father looked at me. *"Patrick must have run too! By the time I returned, he was gone. It took me two weeks to find him.*

"I have a friend on the police force who did some checking. He told me that Patrick was in a shelter. I went to see Patrick, but I wasn't allowed inside. Couldn't see my own son! Imagine that! I went kinda crazy, caused a disturbance, and broke a window. They arrested me. The judge said that Patrick had the right to refuse to see me and to refuse medication, and that I would be prosecuted if I came within fifty feet of the building." He pointed to the sidewalk. *"It's why I stay here in the street."*

Patrick yelled. **"Tom Brocaw eats the same kind of shit we do! They make him. Except, he's rich! He has servants make it into cute little sandwiches first!"**

I watched the father's sad face.

"You can't ignore me, sir! I am a human being and I deserve respect."

"How long do you think he's going to live like this?" the old man asked. *"Ten years? Twenty? Fifty?"* A sob racked his body, and he toppled sideways and grabbed the trunk of the car. For a brief instant, I thought he was having a heart attack and I grabbed his arm to steady him, but he shook me away. Without looking up, he spoke.

"My policeman friend tells me Patrick is getting worse by the day. Of course he refuses treatment. No one can force him. That's the law, you know!"

Before I could comment, he spoke a rush of words.

"See, I have cancer - it's a bad one." He laughed. *"My suffering is gonna be over soon."*

"Oh, God!" I said. "I am so sorry."

Patrick yelled again. **"Cowards die a bazillion times before their deaths! The valiant never taste of death but once, old man!"**

"Don't be sorry for me!" the father said. "Death solves my problem." He nodded toward Patrick, who had retrieved the wine bottle from the trash and had raised it vertically to get a final drop.

"I've been worried about what would happen to Patrick after I passed on. I come here every day to watch him and look at the photos – and remember. He won't talk to me, and I can't touch him – hold him - but I can still do one thing he and the crazy law can't control. I can love him - just like he was five again and sitting on my lap. I tell myself that he enjoys my being here, but I'll never know for sure, and there's no time left for me to find out."

Tears filled his eyes – and mine. He paused

"But who will love my poor Patrick after I'm gone. All he'll ever get from anyone will be disgust and ridicule. Patrick deserves more! I can't force him to be safe and cared for, but I can still love him – if not for what he is, then, By God, I'll do it for what he was."

The man steadied himself on the car, then looked me over.

"So you see, I'm recruiting an army - for Patrick. One person like you every day. Because, when I'm gone, and you're down this way, and you see Patrick, you'll know who he was, and you won't be able to hate him, no matter how bad he seems to want it."

He looked down the street toward infinity before continuing. "Sorry to bother you, sir. Remember Patrick - okay?"

I promised I would.

I had spoken the final few sentences facing the windows and the streets below. When I turned, I noted the tears. Even J. Mark dabbed a handkerchief gently to his eyes. I paused.

"So, good people, I'm proposing a pro bono project. Let's turn the crazy legal code on its ear. Who wants to join an army, and get the Patrick's of the city off the streets and into a safe hospital?"

Every hand in the conference room went up. Susan Jeffers' was first.

She smiled. "Why not? He can make Tom Brocaw twitch!"

SATAN WAS A PATIENT MAN

By Hank Turowski

It started inauspiciously the Sunday after Easter. Eileen had reminded her oldest son, Andrew, to finish his garbanzo beans before taking seconds of tuna helper.

"You don't care about me!" he shouted. "All you care about is my eating beans!" His statement puzzled me, but I chalked it up to teenaged hormones, and continued eating my dinner – beans and all.

Undaunted, Andrew stood. "If you'd pay me more attention and treat me like an adult, Eileen, maybe I wouldn't be flunking so many subjects! Maybe I wouldn't be so disruptive! Maybe I wouldn't be so angry!" Eileen, being Southern, became flustered and couldn't respond.

Then Andrew hit us with his version of a coup-de-grace, "You are the meanest and stupidest parents ever born."

I chuckled, hoping it would end there - while my food was still warm - but it was not to be. Eileen immediately launched into a convoluted story about her Great Uncle Arlo's hand crafted rocking chair. Normally I love listening to her rambling Tennessee farm stories, but I was hungry, so I feigned interest and continued eating.

Andrew knew he had lost the day, and I felt strangely sorry for him He shouted. "I hate this family! I hate your Great Uncle! And I hate you both!" With that, he stormed from the kitchen – without finishing his beans.

Scott, Eileen's other son, twelve-years-old and the most expert glowerer I have ever known, had been quiet to this point. But his jaw had tightened, he was squinting relentlessly, and his eyebrows practically touched his cheekbones – all of which were signals that he was unhappy. He jumped to his feet, and beaming a hateful look at his mother, he marched resolutely from the kitchen.

"And where are you going?" Eileen asked firmly.

"To my room!"

"Why?"

"Because you're mad at Andy, so you'll probably start on me next. I don't want to hear any stories about your family, and I'm just going to get mad. Besides," he whispered, "if I don't support Andy, he'll hit me when you're not looking."

Eileen was too shocked to protest. She shook her head, and auburn hair swept across her gorgeous face. Hoping to avoid what I knew was coming, I ate faster.

Finally calmed enough to speak, she looked at me. "I can't stand it any more!" she moaned. "Every night it's the same turmoil. I would sell my soul for one quiet, decent, and respectful family meal. Like we used to have back in Tennessee."

The doorbell rang. Eileen and I exchanged glances.

"I'll get it," I offered.

The man at the door wore a strikingly red suit and a matching cape that hung loosely at his shoulders. He was stunningly handsome despite the overly-flushed complexion, the odd protuberances on either side of his forehead, and the long, thin appendage that stuck out behind him and shifted from side to side as he watched me.

He was very thin, stood nearly six feet tall, had coal black hair, and a pointed goatee. His smile was engaging, but his eyes - two mysterious dark orbs - made me uncomfortable. My first thought was that someone had gotten the holidays mixed up, and that an errant trick-or-treater had come knocking. But, as I looked closer, I knew I was mistaken. Without speaking, he handed me a business card, and waited.

Fallen Angels, Inc.

Temptations, Retributions, Mischief, and Commodities Trading

SATAN

(Chief Executive Officer)

I sucked in a breath and drew away, then rushed an exaggerated sign-of-the-cross, and said a quick 'Hail Mary'.

I hadn't gotten to the 'fruit of thy womb' part, before Satan laughed, then nodded skyward. "Please, sir. He's not going to listen to you. You're not in such good standing with the Big Guy."

"How do you know that?"

"We talk." Satan snickered. "It's like spiritual E-Mail. He and I share client lists. It saves time and expense."

"Share?"

"Of course!" He looked at me skeptically. "Oh, I forgot. You slept through most of Catechism, didn't you? Let me explain. God sets the rules. You are born pure. Then he lets us do our work while you are alive. He hardly ever interferes – free will and all. We deal in all the delicious human frailties – you know - lust, avarice, enmity." He smiled, then patted my tummy, "Gluttony."

"Hey!" I replied indignantly as I sucked in my gut. "That was a cheap shot!"

He smiled. "In truth, He encourages us. Shares all kinds of information. You know what He says; 'I never give anyone a challenge he cannot endure' – that kind of crap. It's simple, really. No non-tested products ever get into heaven." He winked. "I like to think of us as God's quality control team."

Satan looked over my shoulder as he spoke next. "So, where is she?"

"Who?"

"You know. The Southern Belle! Miss, 'I'm so anxious for a quiet meal'."

"What do you want with her?"

Satan flashed a look of impatience. "Look at my card again," he said slowly.

I did. It had changed subtly. The words 'Commodities Trading' were now red, and the letters seemed to pulsate eerily and smell of sulfur.

"Nice trick, but I still don't get it."

Satan shrugged. "You sir, are a dullard." He spoke patiently. "We lost angels have dealt in commodities almost since the beginning of time, my friend – Our stock in trade is souls. And your dear wife just offered hers in exchange for some peace." He smiled wickedly. "It's quite a trade, isn't it? Perdition for polite conversation? Ruination for respect? Damnation for a decent meal! Such a shame! This should not take more than a few minutes." He leaned in toward me. The smell of sulfur was stronger. "But let me tell you, sometimes it is damned hard. I did the negotiations with that Gates fellow. What a deal he cut!"

"Well, forget it!" I shouted. "She changed her mind. Go away!" I searched my sleepy Catholic School recollections for some appropriate vocabulary. Inspired, I raised my hands and yelled, "I cast thee out!"

Satan stood firm, his ingratiating smile unchanged. "You can't get rid of me that easily. The hostess invited me, remember? You'll need to perform a messy Exorcism. And with the Church bureaucracy the way it is, fat chance getting the Bishop to approve one. But in the meantime..." He glanced over my shoulder. "Good evening, madam. May I have a word with you?"

Eileen had slipped behind me. I turned to warn her, but found I couldn't speak.

Satan handed her a card.

After the Fall, Inc.

Lottery Consultant, Horoscopes, Commodities Trading, Financial Planning,

B. L. Z. Bubba

(Owner)

I turned back toward Satan. He now appeared in the guise of an antebellum plantation owner. He still wore the ill-fitting suit, but now it was stark white and the cape was gone. So were his horns and his tail.

"Financial planning?" I whispered.

He chuckled. "Want some good market tips, sir?" He asked in a voice thick with Southern angst. "There's a price, suh!"

"How do you do, Mister Bubba?" Eileen asked. "Please come in. Would you like something to drink?"

"Why, no thank you, ma'am. In truth, ah can not stay long."

"Are you sure? How about some herbal iced tea? Very refreshing."

"Why ah'm sure your tea is fine, Miss Eileen, really, but I must be off soon."

"Well at least try one of my pecan tarts. Everybody raves about them."

"I don't want to impose, Ma'am."

"I insist!"

Satan smiled. "Your graciousness demonstrates your fine breeding. But just one. I have an appointment with someone high up in national politics. It would be bad manners to say who, but you would certainly know the name."

While he was talking, I had time to notice him more closely. The suit he wore was shabby! His shoes were unpolished! And his shirt had a spot on it. He glanced at me and my voice returned.

"Question?" he asked.

"Your clothes? They look like – Hell?" I chuckled at my play on words. "Why don't they fit better? Why aren't they new?"

He sighed. "You can not imagine how embarrassing it is for the Prince of Darkness to go out in public this way. I used to be considered quite dapper. But no one cares how we are dressed anymore! It simply does not matter. Some of my lesser minions wear jeans and have started something called 'Casual Fridays'. Humans are so hell-bent to condemn themselves for a few extra dollars or a night with a Hollywood trollop, that we have trouble keeping up with the demand. My dark army is all tied up for months. That is why I am here personally to see Eileen. Unless you happen to be famous, you can't sell your soul without a minimum three week advance notice, and most of the really interesting attractions down where I rule – the delightful tortures - booked solid for centuries." His eyes glinted wickedly. "The eternal damnation business is booming."

"Take me instead!"

"What?"

"Leave her alone. Take me!"

"Oh, please! You must confuse me for a lesser minion. Why would I let you undo a negotiation by accepting your selfless act? When your Judgment Day comes, the Big Boss will void our contract to reward you." He chuckled. "He still has the final say, you know!"

"Mister Bubba?" Eileen interrupted. "Please come into the kitchen."

I followed Satan into the kitchen. Eileen had prepared refreshments. There was fresh coffee in the pot, the china cups had been set out, and an assortment of sweets and goodies were arrayed on the table. I could sense Satan's displeasure, but his voice remained calm. "You should not have gone to such trouble, ma'am."

"Why, it was nothing. Just a little Southern hospitality. Please sit."

Satan slipped into a chair and stared at the feast. "Help yourself!" Eileen urged.

The Dark Lord took a small cake – devil's food, I noted - and placed it carefully on his plate as Eileen poured his coffee. "Don't forget the Pecan Tart!"

"Yes, yes! Of course." He added a tart to the plate.

Eileen sat next to me. She picked up her cup and raised it in the air. "I know it's not customary to toast over coffee, Mister Bubby, but here's to a fine visit." She waited, cup poised in the air.

I had an idea. "God bless us, everyone!" I said.

Satan glowered at me, then lifted his cup. I could only imagine how painful it must have been to drink to the good health of the people you are supposed to tempt and destroy. Satan nearly choked as he sipped the hot coffee.

"Hot enough for you?" I asked.

Satan caught the meaning in my comment and flashed a flinty look at me.

I had a sudden uncontrollable call of nature. "Oh, my! Excuse me please!" I rose and hurried down the corridor.

As I returned, I heard Eileen's drawl drifting out of the kitchen doorway. "You see, Mister Bubba, the Continental Congress ceded the land to my father's family after the Revolutionary War. But surveys were inaccurate in those days."

"Yes, yes. Of course!"

17

"'Well, my great, great, great, great granddaddy arrived on the property, the very first thing he did was walk it from end to end and side to side. He knew right off the surveyor had cheated him out of ten acres. He went right back to Philadelphia and challenged the scoundrel. Had a duel and shot the rascal dead. President Jefferson allowed that he would be able to have those ten acres. And that's how we got the rights to the land on the River."

"A delightful story, Miss Eileen. Revenge is as Southern as fried chicken. But if ya'll can get down to business." The Dark Lord reached into his coat pocket and brought out a document. "I have the contract he'ah. Now let me go over the terms with you."

"Civilization requires proper behavior, sir." She continued. "Society demands respect. An unruly family is an abhorrence." She put another cookie on his plate.

Satan ignored her. "You see, Miss Eileen. We at *After the Fall* understand the South. Why, we will guarantee the most peaceful meal you have ever had."

"How could you possible do what you say?" I interrupted. "Armies of psychologists have failed. I believe those boys have Satanically bad natures."

Bubba flashed another look.

My insides churned, and as I rushed down the corridor, I heard Eileen speak. "You know... my Aunt Dixie used to say that it's easier to train a frog to walk on hind legs than it is to manage a difficult child. Have I told you about my Aunt Dixie? She was a feisty one, sir!"

"Yes, I am sure she was, ma'am. Now about this he'ah contract?"

"About my children, sir!"

No sooner had I returned, than Andrew appeared in the kitchen doorway. "Hi mom! Listen, I'm sorry about earlier. I don't know what got into me. I worked ahead in all my classes and I spent the last half hour cleaning my room. Can I do everyone's laundry, please? And when it's done I'll give that old lawn a good cutting."

"Would you like a cookie, dear?"

"Thank you, momma, but I'd like to finish my chores first."

Eileen turned to the smiling Bubba. "He's certainly changed for the better!"

"Why, yes, he has. Now if you will just sign he'ah."

"Scott, too?"

Scott poked a head into the kitchen. "Momma, I tried on the old clothes in my closet and arranged them in order of how much longer they'll fit. I put a stack of too-small clothes and old toys in bags for charity. Do you mind if I skip television tonight and concentrate on my book report?"

"Want a pecan tart, sugar?"

"No thank you, momma. But could I pack some for the charity people?"

B. L. Z. Bubba's voice was smug. "Now, Miss Eileen, you are the Belle of the Old South, but it really is time to sign. Everybody craves something, Miss Eileen, and I know what you need. Southern manners and good hospitality. A return to Tara. If you sign now, I will personally guarantee everything will be as you want, not just for a day, but for a year. Now, how 'bout that? One year of peace! Interesting? Tantalizing? Irresistible?"

"It's to die for!" I said loudly.

Satan hissed!

Horrible pain engulfed me and I nearly fell out of my seat. Eileen stared as if she noticed me for the first time, then she put the pen down and left the room.

Immediately, the pain passed, and I saw Satan looking away. "Sorry!" He said.

"You're sorry?" I asked.

He didn't reply.

"Wait a minute," I said. "You crossed the line, didn't you? It's a free will thing. You can't hurt anyone directly! You can talk us into hurting ourselves or each other, but you can't inflict pain. I'm a dullard, huh? Well, now I know your weakness!"

Bubba laughed. "We'll see. Human frailties are so easy to overcome."

Eileen returned. "Did you two have a nice talk?"

B. L. Z. Bubba spoke. "Yes we did, my dear. Now please sign and I will give you the year of rest you crave."

"Don't sign!" I yelled. "It's all a trick!"

"Sign now!" The Dark Lord shouted gleefully, "and I will guarantee peace the rest of your life."

"Forever?" Eileen asked.

"No!" I shouted. "Not forever! Only till you die!"

Satan pushed the paper forward and put the pen into her hand again. "Here is your glorious Tara, Eileen! Every day of your life! Sign!"

She shook her head. "Why....I can't!"

Satan, no longer in the image of the Southern gentleman, rose threateningly from his seat. Sparks flew from his fingers. The kitchen became incredibly hot. "What did you say?" he bellowed.

"I can't sign!"

"Why?"

"My daddy taught me to always sleep on a contract. I could never sign anything today. Just leave it here and call back tomorrow evening." She smiled. "I'll make some more tarts."

The Lord of Darkness sputtered. The heat returned. The chocolate in my cookies puddled.

Overjoyed, I yelled. "You lose, oven-breath!"

Then my shirt caught fire. Overwhelming pain gripped me and I fell to the floor. Everything went black.

When I came awake, I was at the table, in my seat. Eileen sat next to me and Satan was gone.

"My goodness, but he rushed off," she said. "Such a nice fellow, and a good listener. Southern men are so mannerly, don't you think?" She frowned. "But he didn't try any of my tarts."

I had almost gotten my bearings when the front door opened.

The boys rushed inside.

"Andrew hit me!" Scott yelled, holding an arm to his side.

"Andrew!" Eileen shouted.

"Yeah? Well you spit on me, you little peckerhead!"

"Scott! How could you?"

"He put a bee down my back!"

"He called me a moron!"

"Yee hah!!!" I yelled. "It worked!"

The three of them looked at me like I was crazy.

"What's your problem?" Andrew asked, then stomped down the corridor to his room.

HOT ENOUGH FOR YA?

"I swear to God, officer. Today started fine – just colder. Not the weather, which was hot and muggy – like it oughta be in August. I guess how it is, is like, I **felt** colder –ready to freeze up solid any minute."

Neither of the two cops seemed to understand. Frustrated, I adjusted the collar on the ill-fitting jail coveralls, then continued.

"I mean, look at me now. This here room's hot as a oven, ain't it? But me? Hell, I'm shivering like December. I'm that cold I tell you!"

The cop across from me had taken off his suit jacket. He was a middle aged man, with saggy cheeks and dark eyes sunk into his head like they was hiding. Sweat glistened under his nose. No sympathy. He slapped a palm on the table and shouted. "Don't hand me any bullshit, okay?"

The heat of his anger circled me like a warm coat - an old friend come to visit.

He yelled again. "Were you at the Locust Point Deluxe Theatre this evening around ten?"

I wanted more of his oven-like hate. They thought I was dumb – maybe I was, but I was smart enough. "That's where they picked me up, ain't it?"

His glorious heat washed me again. I started getting excited. I think I giggled.

He leaned toward me across the table. "Answer my question, numbnuts!"

I smiled. "Hot enough for 'ya?"

His anger warmed me again. It had been weeks since I was hot – until today. Weeks? Was it weeks ago the feelings returned?

I remember – the freight yard – at the ocean terminal - standing in the office doorway. The foreman, Mister Murphy, hired me to do odd jobs – sweeping and cleaning mostly. He went to the can, and, like the rest of the crew, I stopped working. I rested on the broom and stared out the open doorway at the grimy scene.

Possibilities   Hank Turowski

    Empty trucks squeaked past the building on their way to the docks, and loaded trucks groaned out the gates. The thermometer outside read 102 degrees. A scorcher! I zipped up my jacket as far as I could. The more the other laborers complained, the colder I had gotten. The more I bundled up - the more they complained - the colder I felt.

    A loud zipping sound startled me. Murphy had returned, pulling up his fly. "Christ Almighty! I can't leave you bastards alone for five minutes. Close that goddamn door, Dumbrowski, and get your butt back to work or they'll be hell to pay!"

    "Come on, Murphy!" The big, Negro fella shouted. "Give us a break! It's way too hot to pull that whitey shit. Ten days of this heat, and my nigger ass is done wilted."

    His wide nostrils flaring like a racehorse, he nodded toward me. "And where the piss did you dig up the retard? Man, I swear. If he opens that door one more time to let out the cold air, I'm gonna tie a truck chain round his neck and fling his puckery blubber ass in the harbor. What the hell's wrong with that boy, anyway?"

    "Yeah, Murph!" the little greaser added. "The guy gives me the creeps. It's a million degrees out, and he don't ever take off his jacket – says it's too cold. You gotta lay him off, for sure."

    They were saying bad things about me. And I didn't hurt them none. I shivered as I felt the cold feelings rushing in - taking control. Panicked, I ran out the door.

    "Hey!" Murphy yelled. "Get your fat ass back here!"

    Too late. The cold had me.

    "Hey, stupid!" The man-cop shouted. "I'm talking to you! What were you doing at the crime scene?"

    "I don't remember!"

    "Ten blocks from your apartment on the hottest night of the year! With no clothes on? And you don't remember? You didn't walk all that way naked, did you?"

    "I suppose not."

    The partner spoke for the first time. She was younger, pretty. But the heat had her too. Her voice sounded tired. "Now, wait a minute, Gary. Let Mister Wick have some time to answer." She studied me with a practiced gaze. "You need some time to think, Mister Wick? You want an attorney?"

"Do I need an attorney?"

Man-cop exploded. "That's not our goddamn decision, asshole! If you want an attorney, say so! If not, answer the questions!"

Ecstasy! He was so easy to control. Warmer, I eased the jacket zipper down a bit and unbuttoned the top button of the jail shirt. "Which question?"

Man-cop started around the room toward me. "You son of a bitch!"

Another button loosened.

But Lady-cop stood in the way. "Wait, Gary! You can't be roughing up any more of the prisoners. You remember what the Chief said last time?"

Man-cop glared at me. I was almost comfortable now. "I don't care, Judy! I feel like strangling the son-of-a-bitch!"

Lady-cop spoke carefully. She was too calm. I was going to have to watch her. "Are you a slow one, hon?" she asked. "Do we need a shrink to check you out?"

"Slow?" I felt hurt. The cold returned. I began to panic.

"Yeah," Man-cop said. "That's it! He's probably a moron! I'll bet he escaped from some loony bin. I'll check the records."

Moron? Sudden freeze! Buttoning up, I moaned.

Lady-cop moved to a closer seat. "Listen hon." Her words carried frost. "Do you remember why you were arrested?"

Shivering, I shook my head violently, trying to force my thoughts backward in time again. "Too cold!"

The patrol car was Arctic. The two policemen had cranked up the air conditioner. It roared poison at me, and I huddled on the back seat, near to death.

"Hey buddy," one of them shouted, "don't be getting sick on me. I have to clean the car at the end of the shift."

The second one laughed. "You're lucky, Tom. This one's a nut case, no doubt about it – probably cracked from the heat. Worse thing - we get a little puke. I don't peg him as a defecator like the scumbag last night."

The first cop laughed as he turned toward me. "You're not gonna puke, are you?" He looked me over, then laughed. "Man, I wish I was naked in this heat."

For days, I stayed in my hotel room. A hundred dollars a week, and all I got was a saggy bed, a battered dresser with a cracked mirror, and a bare bulb overhead. They had turned off the heat, but I kept the window closed and put towels under the door to keep out any breeze. I was almost comfortable, and the feelings had stopped pulling me. That's when the bitch-lady knocked.

"Mister Wick!" she shouted, then broke into horrible coughing. I waited, ear against the door. I could feel her coldness through the wood.

"Mister Wick. I need the rent. Open up please."

Rent? How much money did I have? Not the two hundred I owed.

"Mister Wick. Open up please!"

"I'm sick," I whispered. "Come back tomorrow."

She sighed. "All right, jerk. I'll be back tomorrow alright - with an Eviction Notice and a Sheriff to back it up."

Lady-cop watched my face. I hated her frosty eyes - chilling me inside out.

"Why were you naked, Mister Wick?"

"I dunno. It felt good."

"Where were your clothes, Wick?" Man-cop interrupted.

"I dunno."

"You've been shivering since you got in here," Lady-cop said softly. Her cold words stung my face like ice needles. I pulled away. "It's as hot in here as it was outside. So, how come you decided to take your clothes off at the Locust Point Theatre?"

"Dunno. Just hotter!"

"Why was it hotter, Mister Wick?"

Bitch-lady would call the police and they would take me away. I had to run! But no! I couldn't run! The cold was waiting outside my door.

But if the police got me, their pity and laughter would freeze me, and my feelings would eat me whole. Jokes, laughs, pranks, names. It's how it always started. I had to run. If I went fast enough, maybe I could get warm and the feelings would stay away.

But when I stepped into the dim corridor, the child was there. I think he lived next door. He hated me - I knew it. His fearful glance iced me - deep inside. Child-hate is the worst thing. No hope now. I ran past him down the stairs, stumbling, falling, slamming against the railing. He laughed, and cold air followed me into the street.

"Look, Judy," Man-cop said. "We're not getting anywhere with this dimwit. Let's put him in a holding cell and let the day watch sort him out."

"Wait, Gary. I know Mister Wick wants to talk to us. He just isn't sure how. Right, Mister Wick? Want to talk about tonight? It will make you feel better."

"NOOO!" I jumped to my feet. Shivering, I wrapped my arms around my body.

I had scared Lady-cop. That was good! Her fear comforted me.

Then her face changed, and I knew I was lost before she spoke. "Really, Mister Wick?" she said. "I bet I know what makes you feel good."

"It was too cold!" I shouted. Sudden tears burned my face with frigid water.

"You're plenty sick, Mister Wick, you know that?"

"NO!" I screamed, shivering uncontrollably. "Don't say it!"

"I feel sorry for you."

I froze to my bones!

I left the hotel not knowing where I was or where to go. Inside, the battle raged. Heat and cold. Life and death. And always, everywhere – only the one solution.

The Locust Point Deluxe Theatre was an old building. I liked old buildings. They felt warm. I needed warmth. I bought a ticket with my last five dollars.

It was a wonderful old theatre. I felt warm and happy and whole as I walked the lobby. I approached another patron. "Can I borrow a match?"

He looked me over. "You can't smoke in here, mister."

"I know. It's for later."

He gave me a whole book of safety matches. I didn't need that many, but thanked him anyway.

"You went inside the Theatre, didn't you, Mister Wick?"

I ignored Lady-cop. Memories burned like welcome heat. The chill was leaving. Maybe the cops would leave me alone.

"You were in there when it started weren't you?"

I shook my head to stop her words. "Let me be, damn it!"

"That's where you left your clothes."

The vengeful cold returned.

I didn't watch the show. It was a horror movie. It made me shiver. Instead, I imagined the dark walls and the old warm wood. Then I knew what I had to do.

The restroom had two stalls – both empty. I picked one and went inside.

Lady-cop was right. I did leave my clothes in the Deluxe Theatre - on the floor of the restroom. They couldn't still be there, could they? I mean, it did get awful hot - wonderfully hot - when I struck the match to them.

Cold fled when the flames rose. I kicked the burning clothes against a wall near the trashcan. More flames! Wonderful nakedness! Getting warm! But I needed more!

Feeling wonderful – powerful, I went into the lobby.

Ignoring the stares, I started breaking glass countertops and piling trashcans and displays in front of the entry doors. The attendants yelled but wouldn't approach me – naked like I was. Their fear goaded me. Soon smoke began filling the lobby.

The alarm went off before I had the exits fully blocked. But it would do. I stepped back, along the wall, and watched. I could hardly contain my excitement. It was deliciously painful. People noticed. Their fear was warm and comforting.

"You burned the building, didn't you, Mister Wick?"

Lady-cop was so convincing - she had to know.

Hugging the warm memories, I nodded and unzipped my coveralls - all the way.

"There were people inside the theatre, Mister Wick. Women and children! Some are in the hospital! Why the hell did you do it?"

I laughed. Were they really this dumb? "I didn't want to hurt no body! The cold was killing me! I had to get warm, don't you see? My life depended on it!"

The smile on my face must have frightened the cops. Eyes wide, they watched me. "You can't imagine," I continued as I basked in their fear. "The looks on the faces when everyone ran for the doors, screaming, pulling at the barricades, and piling against each other. Their panic was like a saving oven. Their screams seared me all the way through!"

I had their attention now. Pointing a finger at them, I continued. "When the cold comes, it's how I survive."

ANCIENT MARINER

"Look at that!" Cindy said.

Feet propped on the Harbor Dunes balcony rail, Chris Marshall dropped his magazine onto his lap, then stared between his shoes.

Fifty yards to the east, an elderly figure, leaning precariously forward, labored a flat-bottomed aluminum boat across the sand - toward the ocean. The boat seemed nearly twice the size of the old man. In the background, row after row of blue-green waves rose sparkling in the afternoon sun, poised momentarily, then pounded the rocks and swept hissing foam to the shore.

"I wonder what he's doing?" Cindy Marshall asked.

Chris eyed her for a moment, then picked up the magazine and continued reading.

Cindy nudged his legs with her hip, spilling his feet onto the painted wooden deck. "He'll have a heart attack. Go help him!"

Chris sat up, then adjusted the rubber strap that held his longish dark hair in a foot-long ponytail. "But we came to Maine to rest, not work. Remember!. If we go in September, we'll miss the crowds. Have the beach to ourselves. Recharge the systems."

Still intent on the old man, she moved toward the steps, short dark hair bouncing from the motion. "My curiosity is piqued, my dear." She said. "Let's go. And bring the camera. This has the feeling of a good story!"

Chris hesitated as he watched her retreat down the steps and start across the sand. "Well," he sighed, "she's seldom wrong." Then hefting a nearby canvas bag, he followed. Across the side of the bag in bold blue letters were the words "Chicago Sun Times".

He quickly caught up to Cindy. As they approached, Chris removed a camera from the bag and snapped a series of photos of the elderly figure. Close to eighty - thin framed - slightly stooped - wild white hair chaotic in the sea breeze. Gaining no more than a few inches with each step, the old man relentlessly struggled his boat toward the water. The shush-scrape sounds of his labors dampened even the surf's hiss.

Cindy didn't wait for introductions. "Hi! Can we help?"

The old man stopped. Grimacing, he straightened slowly – the effort clearly painful, and turned toward her. Squinting, he sighed. "Help?" His accent was thick with New England suspicion. "How?"

Cindy pointed to Chris. "Looks like you've got quite a load. My husband used to lift weights years ago. Now, he obviously needs some exercise. He'll pull the boat for you, if you'd like."

Chris regarded Cindy with a brief look, then he too smiled at the old man. "Sure. Happy to help."

The old man seemed reluctant to shed his burden. He stared at the boat, at them, then at the expanse of sand separating him from the water. But shrugging, he handed the rope to Chris. "If 'ya don't mind." Chris took the rope and noted the red welts on the old man's hand from where the nylon had abraded his palms.

Chris slung the rope over his shoulder, and pulled toward the shore. Immediately, his feet slipped, and he fell to his knees on the cool sand.

The old man chuckled. "There's a knack. Short steps. Lean forward. Pull with your legs."

Frowning, Chris struggled to his feet, and studied the boat for several seconds before restarting. Soon, deep, shushing sounds marked each advancing step. "This is heavy!" He announced.

"Reckon so."

"What brings you here?" Cindy asked. The breeze pushed strands of hair into her mouth that she brushed aside as she waited.

"Have to come." The old man answered.

"But why did you bring the boat?" She asked.

"Need to use it."

Unaccustomed to his crisp efficiency of speech, Cindy sighed.

"Can I ask your name, sir?"

"Yup."

Cindy waited several seconds before continuing. "Ah…What is your name, sir?"

"Ryan. Samuel Ryan."

"Well, Mister Ryan, we're the Lawsons – Chris and Cindy. I'm curious; there are other nearby places to launch a boat that are far more convenient. Why here?"

"Have to."

Catching on to the game, Cindy asked. "But why this exact spot, Mister Ryan?"

He stopped and for a moment his eyes watered. "This was where I lost my wife."

Cindy's voice could not hide the confusion. "Lost her?"

"Yup."

"You mean she died here?" Chris interrupted.

"Yup. Out there." He nodded in a seaward direction.

"How long ago?"

The old man paused, closed his eyes tightly, then raised his head skyward. "Thirty years, I reckon."

"And you come back here to remember her?"

Ryan slowed his pace and his face reflected an inner agony. "'Ever year 'bout this time."

"Amazing!" Cindy whispered as she drew alongside Chris.

"I feel like we're intruding," Chris gasped in reply as he labored forward.

"No, no. This is a great human interest story."

Chris watched sweat drip from the tip of his nose. "If I don't have a heart attack."

"Stop!" The old man said firmly.

Startled by the sudden command, Chris lost the rhythm and stumbled. He went down on his knees again.

"This is fine." Ryan said.

"But," Cindy added. "We're still ten yards from the water."

The old man looked along the beach. "Come six AM we'll be knee-deep, I reckon."

Still on his knees, Chris gasped. "So, you're going to launch in the morning?"

The old man squinted into the sky, then nodded seaward. "Tide'll be right. Hardly a breeze. Waves naught to speak of."

Cindy's delighted eyes widened. "Can we watch?" She blurted.

Chris opened his mouth, but Cindy glared him quiet. With that, Chris set about photographing the boat, the old man, the gulls, and the swath of smooth sand left in the wake of his exertion. He felt proud of his efforts.

Mister Ryan regarded them for a long time before answering. "Come along if you've a mind to."

Cindy beamed a smile at the old man. "With you? To visit?"

"Yup."

"But why?" Chris asked. "Shouldn't this be a private thing?"

"It will be!"

The morning dawned bright and cheerful. The weather was perfect, just as Ryan had predicted.

"Did you bring the camera?" Cindy asked, as they hurried across the dark, cold, sand.

"Of course!" Chris mumbled. "But listen, I still feel uncomfortable about this."

"Stop being so crabby!" She scolded. "You know I'm never wrong about these things. This is going to be great!"

Chris huffed. "Great, huh? Let's see. Getting up at five. Shaving when my eyes aren't open. Hotel Restaurant not serving yet. And stumbling in the cold sand to a tiny boat because you think it's a story." He paused. "You call that great?"

She ignored him. "I called Mister Sanborn last night and left a message. I didn't give details – just that we had uncovered a human-interest story that could win the paper a Pulitzer Prize. We came so close last year that he was crazy with anticipation that I call him this afternoon."

"Pulitzer Prize?" Chris scoffed.

"Sure. An eighty-year-old man, so devoted to his wife's memory, that every year he drags a boat twice his size across a half mile of burning sand to brave the cruel ocean so he can 'visit' her. My God! What a story!"

Chris laughed. "Twice his size? Burning sand? Cruel ocean? I think you may have exaggerated the facts a bit."

Cindy ignored him. "There's the boat! Now where's Mister Ryan?"

Chris studied the scene. "I'll be damned! Tide's in. Just like the old fart said."

A shadow arose from within the boat. "I see ya' made it!"

"Of course, Mister Ryan." Cindy answered. "Did you sleep in the boat last night?"

"Yup. Always do."

"Wow!"

Chris snapped another series of pictures - the flash freezing the morning stillness.

"You're sure we're not intruding?" Cindy asked.

"Like the company," he replied.

Then he scanned the pinkening horizon. "Tide'll shift fast!" he exclaimed. "Maxine's waiting. Let's launch!"

The bow of the boat was awash. They pushed it deeper into the easy surf and Cindy and Ryan climbed aboard. Feet immersed, Chris held the boat steady, then shoving off, he climbed in.

Ryan took the middle seat, gripped the oars, and began pulling against the tide. With each stroke, the oars cut deep into the water.

Cindy turned to Chris and questioned him with raised eyebrows.

Chris shook his head. "Want me to row, Mister Ryan?"

"Know where we're going, son?"

"Ah...No, sir!"

The old man laughed. "Then I guess I'll keep at it."

The sea was calm and the boat made good progress. Respectfully quiet, Cindy watched the old man while Chris snapped photos. By the time the sun torched their faces, they had rounded a rocky spit and were out of sight of the Hotel and the beach. Aaron kept on, steering them around and through rocks, some reaching more than twenty feet out of the ocean. Water rose and retreated along sheer stone faces, and kelp just beneath the surface danced the rhythm of the tide.

Aaron Ryan rowed for more than a half hour, then shipped his oars. Chris, who had just fallen asleep, sat up.

Ryan stared ahead, watching the rocks, as the small boat drifted gently. The only sounds were the gentle sweep of water on stone, and the chirp of tiny seabirds roosting nearby.

For more than a minute, old man Ryan stared.

Chris and Cindy exchanged worried glances.

Finally, Ryan turned to them. "Yup. This is it."

"The place where your wife was lost?" Cindy asked.

"This is where I lost her."

The old man resumed rowing, easing them toward a sheltered opening between two sheer rock walls. Above them, rocks dipped ominously low until it seemed there was barely enough room to float under.

"Ah, Mister Ryan!" Chris asked. "There's not much clearance. Is this safe?"

"Safe enough."

The oars scraped the rock shelf as Ryan maneuvered them into the opening. Once through the rocks, the water deepened again. High walls of stone - open to a dazzling blue sky - surrounded them. Ryan pulled hard on the oars and they emerged into a sheltered cove no more than a hundred feet across. On the far side, dark rocks formed flat ledges that gave the place an amphitheatre effect.

The boat drifted across the cove. Ryan used an oar to fend off the rocks and to shift the boat until it was alongside the far wall.

Spryly, the old man, grabbed a small nylon overnight bag, stepped onto the ledge and tied off the boat to a sharp outcropping. Then he reached a hand out to Cindy.

Standing beside Cindy, Chris began taking pictures.

"What kind of place is this, Mister Ryan?" Cindy asked.

"Not a nice place to die." He answered.

"What happened to your wife, sir?"

He stared across the cove. "We found the cove by accident. On our honeymoon. Rented a boat. Rowed around. There it was. The opening. Maxine dared me to row inside the rocks." He laughed. "I couldn't refuse."

He sighed. "Came back every year. Never told a soul 'bout it."

"How'd your wife die, Mister Ryan?"

"I lost her here."

Something in the way he said it, made Chris turn. "What do you mean?"

Samuel Ryan stood, statue-still for several breaths, staring across the cove toward the rocks. He didn't seem to be aware of them. When he spoke it was with renewed conviction.

"Twenty years married. Then she up and turned bad. Didn't want me near her. Always criticizing. Nag, nag, nag! Said she was going to divorce me. Made no sense a'tall. I think it was some mental thing. Even the neighbors were mad at her."

He had spoken so rapidly, that he needed a moment to catch his breath.

"We came here that summer. She didn't want to come, but I insisted. We brought our boat."

He pointed to the rock ledge. "When we got here, she said it was all over. She was moving away. Gave me a long letter telling me I could have a divorce."

Ryan sighed. "I guess I got angry. I yelled, took the boat, and rowed, back to the Hotel."

"You left her here? Alone?"

The old man lowered his head and nodded. "Figured she'd swim out. She was a strong woman."

Cindy's voice became suspicious. "She didn't?"

"I waited a year," he replied. "No contact. Decided she'd run away. But when I came back the next summer. She was still here."

"Still here?" Cindy screamed.

Ryan walked to the far side of the grotto and pointed into the water. "There she is. Every year - waiting for me."

The old man backed away to let Cindy forward.

Below them, five feet down, nearly covered by weeds – bones, a shoe, and a skull peering upward, rocking gently with the tide.

"Oh, my God!" Cindy gasped, then turned and huddled against Chris.

"I guess she tried to swim out. The way the rocks and currents are," Ryan continued, "couldn't get away. Got herself trapped down there."

"You killed her!" Cindy screamed.

Ryan hadn't heard. "I lost her a year 'afore she died," Ryan said. "Wish she had run away."

Aaron reached into his bag and pulled out a pistol.

Cindy gasped. Chris moved to shield her.

Samuel Ryan stared at the pistol, then at them. "Maxine needs company."

"You're going to kill us?" Cindy screamed.

The old man sat on a narrow ledge looking down into the cold water at his wife. He shook his head. "Didn't mean to kill her." Sudden tears sprang from his eyes. "She's lonely. I know it." Then he lapsed into silence.

Chris and Cindy huddled at the farthest end of the ledge. "I think I can swim out," he whispered.

"Too dangerous!" She replied.

"Then what? Just stay here and be killed?"

The old man laughed suddenly. "Get in the boat!"

"What? Why?"

"Tide is shifting. Almost too low to navigate."

Chris helped Cindy in, then stood in front of her. "What now?"

"Don't try to stop me."

"From what, Mister Ryan?"

"Maxine is lonely."

"What?"

"Maxine needs company. And I'm so sorry."

Ryan used a foot to push the boat away from the ledge. "Get going!"

"You're letting us go?" Cindy's puzzled voice sounded weak.

"Done me no harm."

"What about you?"

Ahead of them, an errant wave washed into the opening, nearly exposing a sharp rock bottom.

Ryan nodded toward the opening. "Hurry, girl. Not much time."

Cindy moaned. "Chris! Please!"

Chris watched the old man. "Why us, Mister Ryan?"

Ryan laughed. "Good luck, I guess! I worried 'bout someone finding the boat and searchin'."

Chris shook his head. "Come with us, sir!"

The sound of the shot in the confined space was deafening.

Chris winced and Cindy screamed.

When Chris looked back at Ryan, he had stopped smiling. "Paddle fast, son."

"Why?"

"'Cause I just put a hole in the side. If you plug it, you got maybe an hour. Hurry, and you might make it 'ta shore."

"The boat's leaking, Chris! Leave him!"

Chris grabbed the oars and stroked toward the opening.

"Good luck!" Ryan shouted as they navigated the perilous opening. Chris looked back to see the old man on his perch staring at the weeds and bones.

Chris pulled the oars as rapidly as he could, while Cindy stuffed a windbreaker into the hole.

They heard the gunshot when they were a hundred frantic yards away.

THE MOST BEAUTIFUL WOMAN

Sicily. A beautiful island! It fascinates and surprises me every time I visit. But then, I'm prejudiced. Guiseppi Martini, my great grandfather, emigrated from 'La Sicilia' more than a hundred years ago. He settled in New York and raised ten children. My family came west to California after World War II. That's where I live today, just outside Hollywood. I'm a movie screenwriter, which is a lot less glamorous than it sounds. But I love the Old Country, and I return every year to relax and stay with family.

I didn't come to Sicily to meet women, although I'm still a bachelor. Forty-four and still single? I know what you're thinking, but it's not like that. I date. I have relationships. And believe me, mamma bugs me constantly about finding a wife. But frankly, after dealing all week with difficult actresses and their cutthroat agents, I've become disenchanted with the whole relationship process.

So you can maybe understand my surprise when last week, in Sicily, in a little town named Cappoterra, I met the most beautiful woman in the world. Well, I didn't actually meet her. I saw her. What a vision!

I was eating lunch under a huge red and white Cinzano umbrella at a small sidewalk Trattoria with my cousin Vincenzo. The air was warm and sweet with the smell of jasmine, and I felt incredibly alive and contented the way only Sicily makes me feel. I had just lifted a forkful of pasta, when I happened to glance at a black Alfa Romeo sedan, parked awkwardly near the curb. There she was! No more than ten feet away! Enthroned in the passenger seat! Gazing out the window.

My heart raced, and my breath stopped. How do I describe heaven's profile? I'm a writer, but all I can think of are clichés. Thick raven hair cascaded past her shoulders in waves of lustrous silkiness. Her mouth, slightly parted, was full and sensuous, and blazed a moist crimson in the sun. Long, sensuous fingers tapped the dashboard in time to a song on the radio.

Her face was creamy and flawless, and her features were sculpted perfection. She removed her sunglasses and looked my away. Her eyes, huge brown-green jewels, glittered in the sunlight. I wanted to touch her. No, I wanted to own her!

38

I don't think she saw me. How could she? I was a mortal and she was a goddess. She watched an old woman walk her dog. The goddess smiled – and I almost died. The sides of her eyes crinkled – innocent as a child, and her head tilted just a bit.

"Excuse me, Vincenzo." I rose and started for the car.

Cousin Vincenzo smiled and shrugged.

I hadn't taken two steps before a strange voice yelled at me. "Aspeta! Seniore!"

I turned toward the voice. A handsome and swarthy young man waved at me. "Basta, seniore. Non e buono."

Not good? What did he mean?

"Mi scuzzi." I said trying my best Hollywood smile. "Excuse me. I…"

Ignoring me, he jumped into the car, started it, and drove off. Sudden desperation overwhelmed me. Was that her husband? Somehow, I thought not. I noted the license number then I felt an ache growing in my middle. I had lost something! But I wasn't sure what. Not yet!

I remained rooted in place, squinting down the bright strada for nearly a minute.

"Did you see her, Vincenzo?" I called. My voice held a hint of desperation. Passersby stopped and stared at me. I must have appeared strange; standing in the dirty gutter. I didn't care. I had to meet that woman!

"Si! Cugino mio. A dream!"

"God! I must meet her!"

Vincenzo laughed. "Enrico! Come! Sit! Have you forgotten where you are? This is Sicily. These things are not so easy here."

I turned. "I must meet her, Vincenzo."

My aunt Maria was confused when I handed her the paper with the license number. Her dark eyes regarded me suspiciously. "You want me to find this girl, Enrico? How do I do that?"

"Tanta Maria. You are a very smart woman. You know everyone in Sicily – you can do this for me."

She put her hands together, prayer-like, in front of her matronly bosom. "But, Enrico," she said softly. "This is different. The Carbinieri will not tell me who owns this car, and if I find out, then I will have to inquire of the young lady from her family. It will be difficult."

I took out my wallet and removed a wad of lira. "Here! Bribe everyone on the island. I don't care. Find that girl for me."

Aunt Maria regarded me skeptically as she pushed the money away. "Forty years old and acting like a patzo raggazzo. Is not good, Enrico."

I laughed. "Trust me, Tanta Maria. It is good! E multo buono!"

Aunt Maria shook her head sadly.

I could not for a single instant forget the image of that chance encounter. I became more obsessed with every passing day. Vincenzo and I visited the Taormina beaches, the Siracusa ruins, and the Palermo catacombs, but I couldn't enjoy scenery – not when she was out there somewhere. And after each trip, we returned to the Trattoria in Cappoterra. I was lost, and I could only wait.

It took Aunt Maria three days to find the car, and another two to locate the girl. Overjoyed, I hugged the old woman. "Tanta Maria, you are a miracle worker. I will tell the Pope to make you a saint."

Maria didn't answer. I studied her face.

"When can I meet her?"

She looked down at the tile floor and shook her head. "It is not possible."

I felt as if someone had knocked me to my knees. "Why? Is she married?"

Again, she waited. "No. Not married."

"Then what? I must meet her!"

"I cannot say. Go back to America, Enrico."

But I wouldn't go back - couldn't! I called the studio and told them I was extending my vacation.

Aunt Maria became sadder by the day. Every place I inquired, I got nowhere.

"You may be family, Enrico," she said, "but you are a stranger, and this is Sicily. No one will cooperate with you."

"You think I should approach the local capo?"

Her face tightened. "To do that would be inviting trouble."

"Tell me something, anything, Aunt Maria?"

"Go home," she sighed. I have never seen you like this."

After a week of sleepless nights, fruitless searching, and desperate daily trips to Cappoterra, I found myself in a panic – and I did the unthinkable. I became a thief!

Careful not to disturb anything, I opened all the drawers and cabinets in my Aunt's room. My shame had almost stopped me when I found it - a single piece of paper, tucked between the pages of Aunt Maria's Bible. On it was written an address and a single name – Lucia Delangello. Light of the Angels. I knew it had to be her.

The light went on again in my life. I could breathe. I felt restored.

The house was a stucco-covered villa about five kilometers outside Cappoterra. Tires crunched soft pumice as I parked at the end of a long entry drive beside the five-foot high dark lavastone wall that surrounded the grounds. I went to the open gateway, looked up the road toward the house - and saw her!

Lucia Delangello! She stood in a small garden twenty yards away – surrounded by roses of every color. She wore a simple dress that hung loosely from her soft shoulders. It was white, patterned with yellow daisies. The dress could not hide the voluptuousness beneath it. As I watched, she plucked a wine-red rose from an overhead trellis, and her long legs stretched with the motion.

My knees became weak watching her. I think I moaned.

She held the rose to her nose, sniffed deeply, and smiled.

"Scuzzi," I said a little loudly, "Seniora. Possibile de parlare? Can we talk?"

Still smiling, she stared at me, but did not answer. I thought maybe my Italian was not good enough. Or maybe she didn't speak Italian at all. Could she be visiting from somewhere else?

I started to speak again, but a woman's call interrupted me.

"Lucia! Vienne qua!"

Without acknowledging me, Lucia turned and walked toward the villa.

"Wait! Aspeta!"

"Voloce Lucia! Vienne qua!"

Graceful as a fawn, she pranced up a short marble stairway, and disappeared into the house. In a window near the upper door, I saw a middle-aged woman staring at me. At one time, she had been beautiful. The mother?

I wasn't sure what to do next. I waited at the gate for several minutes and had almost made up my mind to approach the villa, when the woman came outside onto the balcony.

She watched me for a long moment, then came down the steps. Suspicious eyes never leaving me, she continued across the garden, and down to the gate.

"What can I do for you, sir?"

My laughing response must have sounded near hysterical. "Oh. You speak English! Great!"

She regarded me with near hostility.

I thrust my hand through the wrought iron bars. "How do you do? My name is Henry Martini. I live in America, but my family owns several homes in the village of Monteverde near Palermo."

She took my hand.

"I happened to see that young lady a few weeks ago in Cappoterra and have been trying to meet her."

The woman nodded. "Ah. So, you are the one. I am Anna LoPriore DelAngelo, her mother. I told Meritcio not to take Lucia into town. And then, for him to stop to buy cigarettes..." She shook her head sadly. Apparently, Meritcio had committed an offense.

"Lucia is very beautiful. I just wanted to talk to her."

The woman made a slow sign-of-the-cross, shook her head, then sighed. Tears filled her eyes. "You cannot talk to her."

I felt panic rising like bile. "I am sorry. If I have offended you in some way. I did not realize it."

She smiled. "Non fa niente. You have not offended either of us. Your Aunt and I talked and we decided it was best that you did not meet Lucia."

"But why?"

She held up a hand to stop further conversation. She regarded me sadly, then seemed to come to a decision. "Come back this evening at dinner time. Bring your aunt. We will talk further and perhaps you will understand."

I drove the car up the long curving driveway to the front of the villa, craning my neck to catch a glimpse of Lucia. Aunt Maria noticed, but I didn't care.

Anna met us at the door. She and Aunt Maria exchanged a flurry of Sicilian dialect that I had no hope of following, then Anna led us inside.

Tea waited on a coffee table in the living room amid a display of cut flowers. There must have been a hundred roses grouped in vases around the room. The sweet smell was overpowering. A tray of Italian sweets sat nearby. Normally I would have been excited, but my appetite had dwindled as we approached the villa. I was as nervous as I could ever remember being.

Aunt Maria began the discussion.

"Enrico," she said sadly. "I told you that you should go home to America and not think about the girl you saw. I asked that you stop searching. I said that Lucia's family did not want you here."

I felt like a schoolboy - scolded for forgetting his homework.

Anna spoke. "I am not a cruel mother trying to hide her daughter. I have good reason for what I do. Now that you know where Lucia lives, there was no choice but to let you meet her."

I felt overjoyed. "Wonderful! When?"

"Now," Anna said. "She waits for you in the bedroom at the end of the corridor."

"Bedroom?"

"Yes. Go to her there!"

I hesitated, then looked at Aunt Maria. She stared at her hands.

I rose. Anna nodded. And, as I started down the tiled corridor, my stomach bubbled with anticipation.

The bedroom door was open a few inches. I knocked, but no one answered, so I pushed the door quietly, and stepped inside.

Lucia was there, back to me, sitting in a chair facing the window. A bouquet of roses rested in her lap. Her hair had been brushed to one side, and I noted the curve of her long graceful neck.

"Excuse me," I whispered. "I hope I'm not disturbing you."

She turned, regarded me with a curious glance, then looked out the window.

I tried to sound charming. "What out there is so fascinating?"

She didn't answer.

Was she deaf? Was that what they were shielding? But that was no stigma to hide. My confidence grew.

I approached the window. Staring into the garden, I spoke again. "It's quite lovely here."

Then I turned toward her – and caught my breath.

Up close, she was far more beautiful than I had imagined. Every aspect equal measure of pure woman and delightful innocence. And those eyes! I was way over my head. I swallowed and began to panic.

"You are the most beautiful woman I have ever seen." I blurted the words out, but they sounded wrong! Too harsh! Too forward! They didn't come close to what I felt! My face reddened. I was a fool!

Smiling, she regarded her bouquet, selected a rose, deep red, nearly black - and offered it to me.

Oblivious to the thorns, I took the rose, and for the briefest instant, her fingers touched my hand. It was electric.

She smiled, then continued to caress the silky petals with a softness of touch that I instantly craved. God! If she could only touch me that way.

Emboldened, I knelt beside her. "Tell me about yourself, Lucia."

She didn't answer. Instead, she offered another rose – pink like a sunset.

I took it. "Have you lived in Sicily all your life?"

Giggling, she handed me another rose. Yellow, painfully bright.

I laughed. "You like roses, don't you?"

"She can't answer you!"

I looked toward the doorway. Anna and Maria watched. Both were crying.

"She can't answer," Anna said again.

I looked at Lucia, then at Anna. "But why?"

Anna sighed, and her voice wavered. "Lucia is beautiful, as you say - but she has the mind of a three-year-old."

I rocked back on my heels. "How is that possible?"

Anna entered the room. Lucia looked up, her eyes alight with love and devotion. Anna stroked her hair as she answered.

"An accident when she was five. Her brother pushed her into a lake near our summer villa. She was under the cold water a long time. Not long enough to kill her. But long enough to take away her voice and to rob me of my daughter. She has been a child like this for thirty years."

"But..." I indicated her hair, makeup, and dress, with a wave of my hand.

I watched a tear slide down Anna's cheek. "A mother's fancy. I dress her, and do her makeup. It helps me imagine what a beautiful young woman she could have been."

"But she is! Why do you hide her?"

Aunt Maria laughed harshly. "Do not be such a fool, Enrico! Seeing her has robbed you of your senses. Men would take advantage. It is not safe for her anywhere."

I looked at Lucia with a practiced, professional eye. "She may be the most beautiful woman in the world, and she..."

"She is not a woman," Anna said through tears. "She is not even a child."

I returned to California the next day. I felt angry! Cheated! Lost! I could not forget Lucia. Her hair, her face, her graceful body. It was almost as if I had competed for, and won, the greatest prize - then lost it forever.

I waited until I was safely in the house before I opened the package Anna LoPriore had given me. Inside were a dozen Italian sweet cookies, and a photograph - encased in plastic.

It was Lucia – maybe five years old – sitting at a piano - beautiful even then. She was grinning mischievously at the camera. My heart ached as I looked closer.

Because there was something more – a spark in her eyes, a dignity in the way she sat, a power in her hands that touched the keyboard. Here was "The Light of the Angels" the life and spunk and promise – now gone - wasted.

I cried for Anna LoPriore, and for Lucia – and for myself.

BEFORE THE GOOKS GET YOU

Night enveloped the boat, and it was black in the impossibly cramped space. Darker then anything I had ever experienced. And wet – my flight suit was soaked from sweat and from the water that seeped through the planks above me. And unforgivingly tight – I could not lift or move my arms or legs more than a few inches in any direction. Worse still were the violent, unpredictable motions that flung me as the small craft chugged through the South China Sea. I had been sick more than once, and I could smell the undigested food and bile that swirled in the briny puddle I lay in. The Gooks had me, and I was in a hell worse than I could have imagined. Dante's wasn't even this bad.

Ever since the ditching, pain had immobilized my lower back. Deep, stabbing, relentless pain. It was slow murder. I had tried to rub the spot, but I couldn't twist my body enough in the cramped space. And every time I tried, a thrust of agony ripped along my right side.

Someone stomped loudly on the planks not two inches from my head and a voice cried out something harsh in Vietnamese followed by the sounds of laughter. The Gooks had me! I let out a deep sigh and wished – not for the first time in the last two days – that I was dead. And if not dead, then at least a return to the wonderful delirium that enveloped me in the long periods between consciousnesses.

After a moment I was back in the Ready Room with the rest of the squadron. It was two days earlier and I was reading the sports pages of *Stars and Stripes* and waiting for the order to launch our sortie. The Oriskany air conditioning had crapped out again - for the tenth time this deployment - and it was hot as hell in the crowded space. To add to the misery, my flight suit was chaffing under the arms.

Rick Howard sat beside me. He had been my mentor ever since I reported aboard three months earlier, fresh from the RAG. He taught me the shipboard routines and pecking order; and which Wardroom stewards would hold back an extra pork chop for a hungry officer; and how to navigate the dangerous streets of Olongopo City. But mostly he had shared his real secrets – the tricks of the trade he had learned in three grueling deployments to Vietnam - like how to stay alive in combat.

"For God's sake, Merritt," he would say. "Don't get shot down. Because if the Gooks get you, you'll never get out."

The first time he had said that I regarded him skeptically.

His response was to point a finger in my face and speak louder. "I don't care what kind of leadership and moralist crap they told you at the Academy, Lieutenant. The Gooks aren't like us. They don't value life like we do. Christ, you heard the stories. There are still poor bastard Frenchmen held and tortured down there - and that's from the French-Indochina War – twenty years ago. If something happens, either auger in or ride it out to sea. Better a quick death or drowning than Gook torture."

I didn't know where Rick got this intelligence information, but from everything I heard from shipmates and from what I could see on the ship's television, he was right. It was not war like they taught us at Annapolis. There was no Geneva Convention in the jungle. These little yellow people hated us!

Another jolt of pain ripped me out of the memory.

Above me, the Gooks were having a meal. I listened to their singsong cackle. I hated their language – it was ugly – like them.

Food! A faint smell of cooked rice and fish stirred my memory, and I found myself hungry. In the two days I had been imprisoned here, the bastards hadn't fed me, and I was beyond hunger. The only water I had gotten – brackish - had been poured into a crack in the deck above and left to drip down onto my face and mix with the constant sweat that covered me. What I wouldn't give for a juicy Wardroom steak. Or some of that rice. Or a God-damn towel!

Commander Dan Still had entered the Ready Room and strode to the podium. He was a tall man, blond, handsome, and charismatic.

"We'll launch in twenty mikes," he said, as he gripped the sides of the podium tightly. "You've had you briefing, so you know what to do." He paused and regarded each of us in turn. "But there's been a change. Charlie is defending this bridge. Expect unusually heavy flak and missiles from both sides of the valley. It won't be easy."

The boat's engines droned. I came slowly back into reality. It was morning. Faint light filtered in. Hardly enough to see. How long had it been? Two days? Three? Why hadn't they put into port?

Footsteps above, then water came dribbling through the cracks. I eagerly lapped it up from where it splashed against my face. Then a louder splashing sound – and a new taste. Tart! Stingy! Urine! They were peeing on the deck above me and it was mixing with the water. Bastards!

I continued to drink, my mouth slurping against the deck. The Gooks could hear! They laughed loudly.

"Holy shit! Look at the tracers!"

"Quiet down, Hound Dog 7!"

"But do you see that, sir?"

"Sure I see it! Now, can the noise, damn it!"

The bridge spanned a long narrow river valley. On each side, the terrain was covered in verdant greenery. I knew from the briefing that the bridge deck was connected to a substantial concrete base more than a hundred feet off the river. This meant that many bombs would pass under the bridge or hit the nearby water. Water explosions would do little damage to such a massive structure. In order to guarantee a direct hit, a pilot would have to be almost on top of the bridge.

I leveled off over the river and bled altitude slowly until I was not more than fifty feet off the muddy red water. Ten miles to the bridge. I'd be there in less than a minute.

Someone was arguing above me. I could hear a struggle and muted grunts and the sound of angry chatter. Suddenly, one of the crew screamed, and a second later something heavy thudded against the deck.

A new smell assaulted me. Blood!

More yelling, then scuffling sounds, followed by a loud splash to starboard.

What was happening? I couldn't think straight.

Five miles from the bridge, the terrain rose alongside me, and tracers started tracking my progress. There were occasional boats and huts along the river. I opened fire with the 30-caliber guns, holding my finger down on the trigger as I weaved from side to side in the narrow valley. This would shake 'em up.

Rounding a slight bend, I could see the bridge. Things were happening fast now. Steadying the jet, I let loose the missiles, one after another, then dropped even lower. I was out of reach of the SAMs for now, and it would take too long to swing the heavy guns on the hillside. But I had to avoid the small arms.

The F-4 carried a single bomb slung low on the belly of the jet. I lined up. Water on both sides of me erupted in fury as light caliber weapons chased my progress along the valley. My wings took hits and by the sudden sluggishness in the rudders, I knew the tail was damaged. But I was almost there.

It surprised me how calm I felt.

Did the engines slow? What was happening? The small craft seemed to be drifting. In port? Meeting another ship? Fear gripped my throat. Oh, God! This was it! The authorities. I began a confused prayer, but the words somehow escaped me.

50

I flew on, aiming straight at the massive support column until it must have seemed to the Gooks that I was on a suicide mission. The incoming fire stopped briefly as I neared the bridge. Then I released the bomb, hit the afterburners, and pulled back on the stick as hard as I could.

I passed within a few feet of the bridge deck almost at the instant the bomb hit. A shock wave drove me upward like a giant hand and the jet lost the oncoming wind.

The stall warning alarm resounded! Then the engine fire alarm! Seconds later, the missile proximity alarm blared. Looking back, I continued my climb.

The bridge was on fire. Smoke obscured my view, but I must have hit it good.

"Merritt! Check your six!" The yell slapped me awake.

I leveled and turned sharply to the east in one motion – toward the sea.

The turn must have confused the first SAM. I hadn't seen it, but it passed so close off my port side I could read the Chinese writing on its body. It exploded a hundred feet above me, lighting the sky and peppering the canopy with shrapnel.

I looked down. Another Sam rose from a position to the east. I dove at it. Confused, it too passed by. The stick was becoming more sluggish.

"You're on fire, Hound Dog, Five! Hit the silk!"

"Negative! I'm going to try for the ocean."

"You need more altitude, Five. Punch out before you explode."

"Negative! I'm not gonna let the Gooks have me!"

Twisting around, I could see flames coming from the engine compartment, and smoke began to filter into the cockpit. How far to the sea? I tried to remember. Ten miles! I could do this. I armed the ejection seat.

Voices! Someone was yelling from a distance. I was too tired to understand what I was hearing. The Gooks replied excitedly.

I heard a metallic scraping sound, and chains being pulled away from the lid of my stinking prison.

Rick Howard had pulled even with me. I could see him eyeing the damage. "You're in bad shape, Merritt. The tail's shot up and the engine fire is burning through the fuselage. Bail out! We'll cover for you until help arrives."

"This far north? There are no friendlies for miles, Commander. I'll take my chances at sea."

"Roger that!" he replied. "I'll alert the SAR. You'll need five more minutes and a hell of a good prayer."

The jet bucked violently. I fought to control it.

"A chunk of tail just fell off, Merritt. It may be now or never!"

"I'm staying with it!"

"Roger! I'll add a Hail Mary. See that rainsquall ahead? That's the ocean."

"I'll make it!"

"Good luck, Merritt. See you in the Wardroom!" He pulled away just as I entered the clouds.

The light was impossibly bright. Everything was a dark blur. I held my eyes tightly shut as the compartment door banged to the deck.

A shadowy figure leaned over me. Dark clothes. Small features. A Gook! Spittle slapped against my face. He laughed.

One after another, the crew took aim and spit. I was too weak to avoid it.

More voices. Loud. Engine sounds! A small boat was pulling up alongside.

Someone emptied a bucket of water over me.

Heavy footsteps. Figures wearing white.

"All right! Let's be easy with him!"

Americans! Sailors!

Someone leaned over and checked my pulse. "His pulse is thready, but he looks to be okay. Lift him slowly.

Hands jostled me, and I felt myself being lifted. The last thing I heard were the excited Vietnamese voices. Then the pain returned and I blanked out.

I was going to count to sixty before I ejected, but almost as soon as I entered the small storm, the plane bucked a final warning, and I pulled the blast curtain down over my face.

I must have deflected off the canopy as I rocketed outward. It felt like I had been punched in the head. The acceleration lasted for a few brief seconds, then the chute opened and I pushed aside the curtain and looked around. The strong wind was blowing the chute nearly sideways and I couldn't see the surface of the water through the storm. How high had I been when I ejected? I couldn't remember. Cursing, I realized that I'd have to ride the seat all the way down.

Almost too late, I saw the water, frothing under the force of the storm. Way too close! Unbuckling, I pushed away from the seat.

Warm water engulfed me, almost knocking me unconscious. Confused, I struggled to get my raft inflated.

I hadn't been settled for more than ten minutes before I heard the boat approaching. Settling back into the raft, I pulled the 45 from its holster and waited. At fifty yards away, I could see them. It looked to be an old fishing boat. Vietnamese!

They slowed and regarded me. My heart was racing and I could almost feel their tension. Thankfully, it was not a military vessel. If they would just leave me alone, the SAR helicopters would be here soon. Once the storm lifted, I'd be safe.

The boat continued to drift toward me. I could hear the crew yammering at each other. The leader came to a decision. He guided the boat alongside me. I showed them my weapon. They stepped back.

My chances of being seen would be better if I waited in the larger boat. Grabbing the gunwale, I hoisted myself aboard.

The crew regarded me suspiciously.

I tried to smile. "Take it easy! I don't want to hurt anyone."

The leader nodded. Did he understand?

Then the rain stopped. I looked up into the clouds. So did the leader. He looked worried. Would the Vietnamese Military show up?

He yelled and pointed out toward sea. I looked but couldn't see anything.

He pointed again, then moved to the side of the boat and gestured excitedly.

I still didn't understand.

Something hit me alongside the head. I staggered.

The leader made a grab at the pistol.

I remembered Rick's words. 'Don't let the Gooks get you, Jim!"

I held on. They hit me again. And again.

Someone kept kicking me in the back and sides.

I blacked out.

"Boy were you lucky those fishermen came along when they did!"

I stared at the smiling face that leaned over me. A navy Corpsman. I was in an Infirmary. I had been cleaned up and someone had hooked me up to an IV.

"What?"

"Those guys saved your life. They told the interpreter how they found you floating in the life raft. Severely injured. Apparently, you suffered a concussion and a broken back when you ejected. There's marks all over your head and bruises everywhere! They said they took you aboard, hid you in the fish hold, then avoided the bad guys for three days while they headed out to sea to find us."

Something was wrong! This wasn't what I remembered. "But…"

"Take it easy, Lieutenant! We told them thanks. The skipper paid them five thousand American dollars and gave them a case of T-Bone steaks for their trouble. They seemed happy enough."

"But…"

"I know! They saved you life!"

I stared at the Corpsman.

He smiled. "Boy, are you lucky those Gooks got you!"

OUT THERE

The noise was deafening! Dishes rattled. Dust sifted from the overhead lights. The dog ran inside whimpering.

Orville Perkins grasped the arms of his easy chair. Mouth open, his thin gray hair fell loosely onto his forehead and his potbelly jiggled in time with the commotion. A month old copy of *The GLOBE* vibrated off his lap, spreading tabloid accusations across the linoleum floor.

In the kitchen, Enid Perkins held the refrigerator closed with one bony hand, and used the other to keep her gramma's white porcelain water pitcher from toppling

After the noise stopped, Orville spoke. "What the devil was that, Enid?"

Enid shook her head and smoothed her housedress against her thin frame. "Lordie! Don't know, Orville. Suppose one of them Air Force jets crashed?"

Orville stood slowly and went to the screen door. Scanning the night sky, he noted a peculiar red glow toward the west. "There's light out there. Maybe it were a crash like you say."

"Reckon you should you go see?"

Orville scratched his head and considered.

Enid narrowed her pale blue eyes and spoke carefully. "Might find somethin…"

Orville nodded. "Yeah. I 'spect you're right 'bout that. Maybe they'd be a reward if'n I do find somethin."

He went to the old fireplace and removed his shotgun from the rack. After filling his pocket with cartridges, he grabbed his John Deere cap from the mantle, took a flashlight from the kitchen counter, and went outside.

"It looks to be 'bout five mile away. I should be back afore midnight." He paused. "Lessen I find somethin'."

"Good luck, sugarcakes."

The moon wasn't up yet and the woods were dark and quiet – strangely quiet. The flashlight hardly helped. Blackie scouted ahead. Orville could hear her rustling through the undergrowth and thought it would be a good night for 'coon hunting. Maybe he'd get one on the way back if he didn't find something.

They followed the old deer track for the first two miles, but soon had to veer westward toward the swamp. Going was slow in the thickets, and heavy rain the last few days made the earth damp and pungent. Orville sweated.

When he stopped to wipe his forehead, the sweet smell of fresh sap made him pause and look around.

Bits of branches were strewn about the ground. Shining the light upward, Orville noticed that the tops of the tallest trees were missing where something had clipped them along a narrow path leading toward the swamp.

Orville studied the debris. "Would you look at that, Blackie!"

The dog whimpered.

Orville studied the dog. "Something ain't right. Is that it, girl? Unnerved, Orville continued on, glancing up occasionally at the damaged trees.

After another quarter mile, clouds of mosquitoes surrounded them, and the trees in the swath were cut almost to shoulder level. Shattered pitch pines littered the ground. Blackie growled and would not explore ahead.

Stopping to survey the damage, Orville swatted at the buzzing nuisances. "Somethin' got ya skeered, girl?" Shivering despite the heat, he chambered two cartridges before moving forward slowly.

He smelled Bad News Swamp before he saw it. "God-awful place!" he mumbled. Blackie began slinking behind him. Orville was wary now.

The edge of the swamp was a mess. Something had disturbed the wet soil, plowing a trough more than fifty feet wide through the earth until it merged with the putrid water. The smell of rotting swamp muck was almost unbearable. Orville choked.

At the edge of the tarn, Orville swept his flashlight over the water, and whispered. "Something big out there, girl. Must be buried in the mud." He surveyed the scene carefully, but aside from the damaged landscape, there wasn't much to see.

"Shucks, Blackie. We wasted a trip."

Then he heard the sound. Deep, rumbling, getting louder, disturbing the water. His flashlight speared the night – revealing the frantic love jitters of a thousand insects.

The rumble grew, then the swamp suddenly erupted in a burst of trapped air. Muck and putrid water splashed them.

"Dang it dog!" Orville shouted. "We'll need a bath for sure."

The pond water settled sluggishly. Orville looked a final time - something was floating thirty feet away – a body?

"Fetch it, Blackie! Come on girl."

The dog was reluctant to enter the swamp. Orville nudged Blackie under the ribs with a muddy boot, then yelled. "Get out there, ya hear!"

The dog cast a sad glance at Orville.

"Go on. Git it!"

Blackie sloshed up to her belly, and whimpering, looked at Orville again.

Orville shouted. "Git that dang thang!"

Blackie jumped out into the deeper water and started swimming.

Sinking her sharp teeth into the material that covered the figure, the dog began pulling toward shore.

It was clear to Orville that the dog could not drag the body out of the mud. Signing, he started in - slogging until he was knee deep.

Blackie pulled the body to him, and Orville dragged it the final distance to shore.

Even coated with muck and strands of vegetation, Orville could see something was wrong – but what? He prodded the corpse with the toe of his book, then shivered again. No hair. Awfully small. He looked closer. The hands! Only three fingers on each hand - very long - way too thin.

Orville frowned. Was this what he thought it was? "Lord Almighty!" He heard himself whisper. "We done catched ourselves one of them aliens!"

He pondered, then, smiling at the dog, he spoke aloud. "We gonna be rich right soon, Blackie. If'n we keep this here away from the Government."

Orville nodded. "Come on Blackie. We got to get home right quick."

The dog had not approached the body and would not come when Orville called. The old man hefted the figure onto his shoulders. It was surprisingly light.

Blackie perked up. She seemed eager to get away. "Good girl! Lead me home!"

Faint noise on the far side of the swamp made Orville pause. Searchlight sweeping the water, a helicopter was approaching from the far shore three miles away. Orville was puzzled. "That thang's mighty quiet, Blackie."

Suddenly afraid, he entered the muddy water, ankle deep and started running quickly south.

"Come on girl. Let's follow the crick home. Throw 'em off the scent."

Two hundred yards away, a shallow creek emptied into the swamp. Hidden by overhanging cypress, it was difficult to see even in the daylight. The helicopter was nearly overhead by the time he reached the canopy.

Huffing, Orville waited until the machine had passed on, then maneuvered around the big trees to the creek bed. Then, staying in the water as much as possible, he trudged toward home.

Enid answered his quiet knock. Staring at the unmoving form, slumped over her husband's shoulder, she pressed a hand to her thin lips and whispered. "Lord Almighty, Orville. What did you bring home?"

Orville brushed past her. "Our ticket outta here, Enid."

"It's a body, Orville!"

"I know that, Enid."

"It ain't human, is it?"

"Don't rightly know fer sure." He laughed. "But it ain't from around these parts."

"Is it alive?"

Orville paused. "I ain't sure 'bout that either. I'm gonna clean it up and find out."

He headed toward the bathroom. "Get the tub ready, Enid. Blackie, me, and this'n here need a good washin." A sudden thought came over him. He stopped. "You take the pickup into town and buy Polaroid Film at the 7/11. Get as much as 'ya can. Use the cookie jar money. This here is like Rozwell, Enid."

By the time Enid had returned, the two had finished washing. The gray-skinned figure lay on their bed, face up. A silvery material covered the body head-to-foot. "It's alien, sure 'nough, Orville!" Enid exclaimed. "I seen pictures in *The Star.*"

Orville loaded the Polaroid and took a photo. Counting, he stripped away the picture to let it develop, moved to the side, then took another.

"The Government's gonna be mighty riled at us, Orville."

Orville laughed. "Only if'n they find out."

"They's everywhere, Orville. Emmy says they can watch us through the television."

"Emmy Wilson don't know nothin 'bout nothin!"

Enid stared at the body. "Is it dead, Orville?"

"Far as I can tell. I couldn't hear no heart and no other sounds inside it."

He took a closer photo.

"How do you know where the heart is, Orville?"

"Just guessed."

Orville had taken a pack of photos before Enid spoke. "He don't look dead, Orville!"

Orville considered. "I suppose we could cut him up to see what makes him tick."

"I don't think we should do that, Orville."

"Why not?" Orville snapped.

"Well, for one thing you don't rightly know if he's dead. He might be a bit riled if you started a-cutting. For another thing, that's our wedding bed he's lying in, and I don't want no un-baptized alien soilin it. It ain't right!"

Orville spread the photos onto the kitchen table. "Okay, Enid. But we gotta do something, otherwise we ain't gonna get no big reward - and no movie contract."

Suddenly Orville looked up. "I got it, Enid. The million-dollar idea."

Enid ran a hand through her stringy hair and stared past Orville at the body in the bedroom. "What is it sugarpie?"

"We'll pretend he ain't dead."

Enid frowned. "How we gonna do that, Orville?"

"We just gotta pose him and take pictures."

"Live pictures? Of a dead alien?"

"They's Polaroids, Enid. Ain't no one gonna know the difference."

Enid was skeptical. "If you say so, Orville."

Enid loaded the camera and Orville posed the figure sitting at the table, staring at the television, and leaning into the refrigerator. Enid took several of Orville and the alien together like they were discussing politics or such. Fifteen poses in all.

Orville examined the photos. "We need something more, Enid."

Enid watched Orville. A huge smile lit his face revealing all the missing teeth.

"Take off your clothes, gal!"

"What???"

"Sure! What is it all them newspapers want? Sex! We'll tell 'em the alien had his way with you, and I snuck up and got the pictures. Lord, you'll be the most famous woman in the world."

"Are you sure, Orville? You know I don't like being in the altogether."

Orville smiled. "Don't you worry none. I'll make the pictures real artsy like."

Ten minutes later, Enid lay naked on the bed beside the tiny figure.

Orville circled the room trying to line up the best photo angle.

"This ain't gonna work, Enid. Can ya put one of his hands on ya somewhere and look scared."

"Lord, I am scared!"

Orville almost yelled. "I got it, Enid. Let's get that uniform thing off it."

"The clothes?"

"Sure, Enid. How we gonna convince 'em you were spoilt if it's all dressed up?"

"But…"

"A million dollars, Enid."

Enid fumbled at the seams of the shiny clothing. "I don't see how this here cover comes off, Orville."

Orville took a Buck knife from his pants pocket. Deftly he slit the fabric from neck to crotch, then stepped back to take another photo.

"Okay, Enid. Get his clothes off."

Enid began to peel the fabric away from the body. "I don't like this, Orville. He don't feel right – he's all spongy."

"Come on, Enid. This is our big chance."

The material came down off the arms, the chest, and the waist. Stopping, Enid looked up. "He don't have no thingy, Orville."

"That don't matter. Nobody knows but us."

"But how can he…. you know…. without a thingy?"

"Lord," Orville answered. "I'm sure I don't know. But you read the stories. These fellas is always makin babies with Earth women."

"I guess so."

With the material down past the knees, Orville carefully lifted the body onto Enid.

"Orville! I'm afraid! He smells funny."

"That's just Bad News Swamp. Quit wiggling and look scared." Orville moved around the bed and took five more pictures.

The sun was nearly up when Orville pronounced the photo shoot a success.

"Now, let's bury him."

"But."

Orville shook his head. "Lord, Enid. Can't you see he's dead? If he was alive, he'd a done something - what with you naked and all. Nope! He's a gonner for sure."

"Well, okay. If you say so."

Orville smiled tenderly. "I know it's been hard for you, Enid, but you'll see, it was all worth it. You stay here. I'll do the burial."

"Do it proper, Orville. The Bible's on the mantle."

Enid had addressed the envelope to *The GLOBE* in bold letters. Inside, was a set of ten photos. Not the best ones, but just enough to let them know, they were dealing with the real thing. Orville called them teasers. He said they'd have to pay big money to get the real things. He whistled as he waited for the postman to take the letter, then he continued on to the General Store.

"Hey, Orville!" Rastus Boteller shouted as he entered. "I hear they's big doings up you way."

Orville feigned surprise. "What do you mean, Rastus?"

"My God! Are you deaf? Didn't you hear the ruckus last evening?"

"Well, seems as I did hear something. What was it?"

"Lord, it was the crew working."

Orville frowned. "Crew?"

"Ain't you heard? They's making a movie over your way. X-Files III or some such. I seen that pretty redhead over here yesterday."

Orville felt his heart begin to pound. "X-Files?"

"Sure. They hired some local boys to chew up the land by the swamp and make it look suspicious. That's what all the noise was – heavy equipment!"

"But, why at night?"

"They was fixin to do a night scene I take it." Boteller snickered. "Then they lost the bodies."

"The bodies?"

Rastus laughed again. "I heard they was loading a crate on a skiff and this big box fell overboard. It had all these rubber aliens inside, and it went straight to the bottom. I doubt they gonna find it, least not in Bad News Swamp they's not. They had to quit workin on your side of the swamp and they went over to the other."

"Is that what them helicopters was doin on the other side?"

"I suppose so. How'd you know?"

"I heard 'em."

Boteller shook his head. "How about that? A movie right here in Cornersville."

Orville swallowed hard. "Right nice, Rastus."

"I can see it now. We gonna be famous, Orville!"

THE BEAST THAT MASTERED SNAKES

The old man moved slowly over the rocks, cautious, but with the gentle grace of one born in the cold mountains. *Enemy of the Moon* the tribe called the peaks, for in the fullness of the night, the mountains seemed spearheads in a dark void, jutting forth to rake the moon and bring demons and spirits falling in terrible moans of agony.

Anger consumed the demons now, and the night winds that tossed his long gray hair into his face, brought eerie screams from the blackened heights. He adjusted the bear skin more tightly around his thin frame. He knew spirits surrounded him, but he also knew he was protected. The shaman had given him a special talisman, a magical figure of coyote bones and shreds of rabbit skin to keep him safe.

His foot dislodged a rock and sent it skittering down the steep, dark slope. The old man could not see the rock, but rather imagined it hurtling into the waiting chasm. He stood like a stone until he heard the rock shatter many feet below.

A smile stretched his ancient lips. The talisman would protect him from the spirits that roamed the mountains, but it would not save him from the mis-steps of an old fool. He must be more careful, for his mission was most critical to his tribe, and perhaps to all the tribes on the western side of the great mountains.

The wind howled again, nearer at hand. He gazed toward the source of the sound, knowing he could not hope to see the spirit that hovered close by, but he was alert nonetheless. Other things roamed *Enemy of the Moon* in the dark. Things not of spirit, but of flesh. Things that would devour him if he were not doubly cautious.

He waited until he was sure no beasts had caught his scent, then, using his spear as a cane, he proceeded slowly upward. The pass was just above him somewhere. He had been through this way many times in the light of day, but now, with no moon to guide him, the play of dark within shadow made the path less obvious.

He came upon a rock he did not remember, and stopped again. His old fingers traced the contours, slowly, gently, then he smiled again. *Old Squaw Rock*! He had strayed from the path nearly twenty paces. Just beyond the rock was a sheer drop to certain death.

He sat, back against the rock, and studied the stars. They were as brilliant as he had ever seen. "Hunting Man" was rising above *Enemy of the Moon*. He remained perfectly still, watching Hunting Man until the last star - the speartip - hove into view above the dark peaks. As he reckoned time, the moon would rise soon, making travel less risky. He would be able to get to the place at sunrise, but he could not rest again.

He retraced his steps until he came to the path. How could he have missed the turn? The howls came again! Probably it was the work of the demons, tricking his senses. He wanted to laugh into the night air. Did they not know he was the best tracker in the tribe? And that he carried the talisman? Demons could not trick him – at least not again. Hunching against the wind, he plodded upward – immune to the howls and sure of every step.

"Hunting Man" was well down and "The Owl" had reached zenith when he arrived at the promised spot on the far side of the pass. The trek had been arduous and his breath came in ragged gasps, swallowed by the winds. In Council they had argued that he was too old for the journey - that they should send a younger brave. But he had made it, and the younger men would not have - none of them. They would have fallen, or been attacked by mountain cats, or gotten lost among the cold peaks.

The evening before, he had waited around the campfire, letting the younger braves have their say. Since he was nearly an elder, he spoke last – as was his due.

When he stood before the Council, he had pulled his back erect. He wanted them to hear his words and not notice his tendency to bend slightly at the waist.

"I have served the People for many seasons. I was a warrior with many of your fathers who have since gone to greet the Great Spirit. I led the War Party that defeated the Eagle People and returned the stolen women to the Tribe." He paused, then pointed across the campfire towards where they all knew *Enemy of the Moon* stretched skyward.

"I was born in the bosom of *Enemy of the Moon*. My mother went high up with my father to hunt elk. She was early with me when she left, but the snows delayed their return - and I was born. Am I not called 'Child of the Mountains'." He stabbed a finger again toward the peaks. "That is my home. No one here, including the young warriors who have bravely spoken, know *Enemy of the Moon* as I do. I alone can claim that place – as I alone can claim this journey. I will do what the Council wants!"

The Council was not pleased, but they could not deny him his request. The mountains were his birthright. True, he was old and slow, and had not been across the mountain in many passings, but after a brief discussion, they had affirmed his right.

The Shaman had given him the talisman, and he had almost refused it. He knew he would be safe in the mountains. He had traveled *Enemy of the Moon* from end to end, and the spirits would respect 'Child of the Mountain's' right of passage. But even so, the talisman would be great magic in this journey.

In the palest hint of pinkening dawn, he climbed carefully downward over hard scrabble until he came to the wide ledge in the rock. The one that was not there at his last crossing. The one the Council had said he would find. He paused and considered. This was something new to him, something alien, something that should not exist, and he was afraid as no mountain spirit had ever made him.

The rock below him had become a sheer wall, hewn from the mountain to twice the height of a grown warrior. It stretched in both directions in a wide path until it turned and followed the curves of the mountain. The wall ended at a level rock shelf, twenty paces wide. Beyond that the mountain again descended to the valley a day's journey below. It was still too dark to descend to the ledge, so he pulled the skins around him and waited, allowing his eyes to adjust.

In a few minutes the light improved, and his heart began to pound against his chest. Lying in the center of the path were two dark snake things – just as the Council had predicted.

But these serpents had no head or tail, instead they lay, thin and deadly, stretched as far as he could see along the path in the downward direction, and passing around the bend in the other. Longer than any snake the old man could imagine.

He could not stay where he was. To fulfill his mission, he must climb down to the ledge – to the snakes.

Carefully, he searched the rock wall and soon found a way to the bottom. Once down, he wasted no time. He crept to the serpent and knelt beside it. Now he could see the two snakes, never touching, lying together on a bed of rocks and hewn trees. Were they mates? If he touched one, would it awaken and devour him?

He removed the talisman from his pack. Reverently, he adjusted the bones and skins to match the complicated pattern the shaman had show him. Then he lay the talisman on the nearest snake. As he did, his hand came into contact with the serpent, and he pulled back, frightened. The snake was cold and hard – colder than death could ever be, and harder it seemed than *Enemy of the Moon* itself. His touch was ignored - the snake slept on.

Despair filled his heart, as the old man crept backward to the stone wall and waited. Since the Council was right about the snakes, they must also be right about the great beast that would come at dawn – the one he must fight and defeat. For the first time in the journey, he felt cold – deep to his bones. His eyes never leaving the snakes, he huddled against the rocks as the sky brightened by small measures.

Not many breaths later he heard the faint noise, far to the south. It echoed like the wail of a lost soul, yet with a voice more powerful than any mountain spirit. Long and cold came the sound, coming louder as the old man listened. Was the beast approaching? The old man felt renewed fear, and tightened himself into a bundle. Murmuring, he asked *Enemy of the Moon* to protect him against this horrible thing that approached. The wailing sounds increased.

The noise ceased abruptly. Was the spirit gone? Had his entreaty worked? Did *Enemy of the Moon* have greater power than this new threat? He watched the two great silent snakes, each no thicker than his arm. They had not stirred at the new sound. Were they waiting?

The sun strained to rise over the eastern horizon when the new sounds came. Great heaving gasps, somewhere around the mountain, like some giant animal struggling up a steep slope. And then he heard a new sound, at a pitch so high he had to strain to hear - a constant screech of agony – and it approached. For the first time, the old man wondered if he should not climb to safety and hide among the rocks. But no! He was a warrior! He would do as the Council asked. He would fight the beast.

The sounds grew in volume – chuffing – like the buffalo running in a winter field, but louder than any buffalo, and the screeching echoed among the rocks and hurt him down in his bones. Now he could feel the vibrations in the very rocks of *Enemy of the Moon*. Such a powerful thing coming that even the mountains trembled.

The Talisman! As he watched, the snakes seemed to awaken, to vibrate with the mountain, and the Talisman wiggled against the motion - and fell off! The sounds of the beast increased. It came for him!

The old man let his eyes drift toward the bend in the mountain where the beast must surely emerge. He was truly afraid, and this confused him. He could not remember feeling fear before. But he could not fail the Tribe. Bent over by the power of whatever approached, he crept on hands and knees toward the snakes.

The Talisman felt good and clean, in his calloused hands. He tied it against his spear with a small piece of antelope sinew. Then the beast roared into view not 100 paces away.

It was enormous, bigger than any bear, bigger than any buffalo, bigger even than some of the rocks that lay strewn about the mountain. It was black as night and had one shiny eye, bright as the sun - an eye that found him and stretched his shadow in a long dark line beside the snakes. When he saw how the beast traveled, he nearly fell to his knees in despair. The black beast rode the snakes, its great round legs spinning, spinning. And the snakes screeched protest but could not rise up against so powerful a thing.

Doomed, the old man accepted his fate. He adjusted the Talisman, then stood, and straightened as best he could, ready to face his death and go to the Great Spirit as a warrior. He loosened the skins and let them fall to the ground so that he was free to battle. His frail sinewy body strained and every taut muscle stood out in stark relief in the harsh light Spear pointed toward the thing, he stood beside the cold snakes and waited.

Seventy paces, fifty, twenty. The light blinded him and he raised his free arm to block the beam so he could aim true. Great balls of smoke rose from the body of the beast as it chuffed toward him blackening the sky in its wake. He found himself smiling. This would be a battle they would sing about around the campfires – but no one would know of his final bravery. He would face his death alone.

A sudden blast of noise! It was the wailing sound, but closer, everywhere, all through his head. He leaned backward away from the sound, gauged his distances, then pointed the spear with two hands.

The sun rose completely as the beast surged forward, blinding, screaming, screeching. He thrust his spear and it was blunted aside by a force so great he could not comprehend what had happened. Thrown sideways, he toppled in a heap against the stone wall, and the beast screamed past him.

Dazed and deafened, he put his back to the wall of stone. Behind the great smoky beast came other shapes, huge and horrifying, one behind the other – all with openings, lighted from within. Figures peered at him through the openings. And still the snakes screeched - deafening him as the beasts passed. He huddled against the wall and watched.

Soon the end came, a smaller thing with a platform at the rear. On the platform stood a man, but not one of the light-skinned horse soldiers the tribes had been talking of. This man was not a warrior - that much was certain. He was fat and wore clothes of cloth and wool and a red cap, smeared with dark. He watched the old man, then leaned over the side of the platform and yelled. "Stupid Indian! Watch out!"

The old man did not know the words, but he understood the derision in the voice, and he remained unmoving until the beast chuffed around the mountain bend and was lost in the distance.

Despair swept over him, and for the first time he noticed the spear he still held tightly in his grasp. The ash shaft had been broken cleanly and the Talisman had been cast aside like a rag. Tossing the spear down, he crawled to the snakes and picked up pieces of the Talisman, careful to keep them together in his pack. He had no fear of the snake-things now. They had been tamed by the beast and no longer had any power.

He entered camp late the next day. Since he was silent, no one spoke to him, and he did not pretend to hold his back straight, for he felt weary beyond imagining. He went to his tent and crept inside to rest. He would bring the news of his dishonor at the evening campfire.

The fire seemed particularly strong that evening, and, as was custom, the Council waited until the warriors had all eaten before addressing him.

"'Child of the Mountains'," the Council Chief asked. "What is this news you bring the People?"

The old man stood, stretching his aching muscles as he did so.

"I have done what was bid," he said. "I crossed the *Enemy of the Moon* at the high pass and brought the Talisman to the place where the mountain was cut raw. There I found the snakes without heads or tails."

Many of the warriors gasped at this news. The Council Chief nodded.

"I put the Talisman on the back of a snake where it could capture the sun, and waited for the beast."

This time there were grunts of approval.

"But the great screaming beast came along the backs of the snakes to contest what I had done. It was bigger even than the Council tent. We fought, but the beast was too strong – stronger than all the warriors of the Tribe together. It broke my spear and crushed the magic from the Talisman."

Now the warriors became angry.

"It is true!" the old man shouted. He dumped the remains of the Talisman at the feet of the Shaman. "It defeated me and the Talisman." He paused. "But there is one more thing I must tell the Council."

Again the Chief nodded.

"The beast was ridden by the light-skins," the old man said slowly.

The Council Chief spoke to the other Council members. His voice was solemn. "Then, the pale ones have come over the mountains?"

Breaking etiquette, one of the youngest warriors stood. "We shall fight!" he shouted.

"If you fight, we all will die," the Council Chief said. "We have heard the stories from over the mountains. They are too many, and their magic is strong."

"I saw many, many faces inside the beast." The old man added. "More persons than the whole Tribe."

"What can we do?" asked one of the elders.

The Council Chief thought for a moment, then replied sadly. "We can only make peace and hope they let us keep our lands."

"I am 'Child of the Mountains'," the old man said. "The mountains are mine, and I will go there."

The Council Chief stared at 'Child of the Mountains' for many breaths. "What safety is there in the cold stone hills?"

The old man shivered. "Perhaps none. But I saw the pale ones and I endured their mocking stares. I do not think we can wait in the rocks until the paleskins have passed us by. I do not think we can live in our lands in peace."

"And if you die there among the rocks?"

The old man laughed. "Then I will die in the arms of "Hunting Man" and "The Owl" will take me safely to the Great Spirit as is our right."

The Council Chief nodded. "Go to *Enemy of the Moon* old man, and take any who will follow."

WHISTLER

"Wanna buy a smile, Mister?"

"What?" The gruff looking man peered down at the small blond haired boy. "What did you say?"

"Wanna to buy a smile?"

The man shook his head sadly, then glanced at his partner. "What'll they teach 'em next, huh Charlie?"

Charlie glared at the boy. "Go away, kid. We're busy – right, Stan?"

"I'll make you smile for a quarter."

Stan almost shouted. "Beat it!"

"I'll make you both smile for fifty cents."

Stan glared at the boy, then turned away. "So, what do you think old man Leet is going to do with our proposal?"

"Probably toss it," Charlie answered.

"Yeah! And if he does?"

Charlie grunted. "Then we're dead, pal."

Before Stan could speak again, they both heard it. A squeak? No. More like a squeal? No. Closer to, but not quite… a whistle!

They looked around, then down.

The boy, stood on tiptoes and puffed his cheeks. His face had turned red as he tried to whistle. He took a deep breath, then blew again. The strain made his eyes cross a bit, but the tinny sound was no better.

Frustrated, the boy puffed harder and his eyes crossed further.

Stan watched, until he felt something unexpected. He started – to smile - then to laugh. Charlie did the same. Soon they found tears flowing down their cheeks. Their laughter went on far longer than the boy's attempted whistle.

When they finished, they found the boy watching them, a delightful smile stretched across his small face.

Slowly, the boy raised a hand, palm out. "Fifty cents, please."

"Now, wait a minute…," Stan began.

The tiny hand held steady. "It's for charity, sir. Sister Magdalena said we should use our talents to help the poor. I don't have talents, but I can whistle."

Charlie laughed. "You sure can.," and reached for his wallet. He put a five-dollar bill in the small hand. "That laugh was worth five dollars, son."

"Thank you, sir!"

Stan handed oven ten dollars. "Boy, did I ever need that! What's you name?"

"Scott, sir."

"That was great! Thanks, kiddo."

Scott stared at the money. "Thank you, sir!" He put the bills into the pocket of his jeans, then looked further down the block. "More smiles coming up!" And trotted away.

The men faced each other. "I haven't felt that good in years, Charlie. What say we forget about old man Leet and take the afternoon off?"

"I'm with you, Stan."

Further along the street, the boy came upon a heavyset woman carrying bags of groceries to her car. Beside her was an older, boy – dark-haired and chunky, who glared hatefully at his mother, then at little Scott.

The woman put the bags on the hood of her car, then turned toward her son. "Do you have any idea how much you just embarrassed me in there?" she whispered harshly.

The boy snickered and his eyes flashed defiance.

The woman grabbed him by the lapels of his jacket and shook him. "I can't take you anywhere! When we get home, I'll give you a spanking you'll remember forever."

The boy continued his defiant look. "Go ahead! I don't care."

The woman rocked backward, gasped, then raised her hand.

The sound stopped her. Not a squeak! Not a squeal! A whistle!

Ten feet away, Scott puffed furiously, eyes crossed and face red.

She watched.

Her son laughed first – a deep laugh – so deep his knees buckled. Confused, she held the convulsing form to keep him from falling.

The little boy continued to blow – a whistle, but not a whistle.

The woman gaped at her son, and – a smile bloomed on her face. Soon she laughed too.

After she wiped the tears, she noticed the small boy, hand extended.

"A laugh for charity?" the little boy said.

Her son took a quarter from the pocket of his jeans and gave it to the boy. "Man, that was worth it!" Then he looked at his mother. "I'm sorry, mom!"

The woman found new tears in her eyes as she fumbled in her purse. She opened her wallet, and then laughed. "My, God! I'm crying so hard I can't see anything. Billy, hand the nice boy a dollar."

Billy took out a five-dollar bill, looked cautiously at his mother, winked, then gave it to Scott.

Farther down the block, a man sat with both feet in the gutter. He looked tired. He was also dirty. And he smelled funny.

"Go away!" he yelled, sweeping his arm in a wide gesture of dismissal.

Scott stood his ground.

The man stared hard at the boy, then noticed a tip of green currency peeking out the small pocket.

"What you got there, boy? Money?"

Scott nodded.

"Man, I need money bad." He reached into his coat pocket and pulled out a handful of change. "See? This here is all I got! Ain't enough so's I can eat. I can't get no room. And I sure can't get me a drink."

The boy continued to stare.

"What you want from me, anyway?"

"Money!"

The man laughed, showing a mouth of missing teeth and ugly sores. "You want money from me? Now that's a good one!" He held up both hands and feigned fear. "You robbing the wrong man, son."

"For charity!"

"What?"

"The money is for the poor."

The man laughed again and spittle flew from his wide lips. He raised an arm. "Now who you think is poorer than me? Why don't ya jus give it right to me?"

Scott shook his head. "Sister said…"

The man growled. "Get outta here. I ain't got nothing you want."

Scott took a breath and stood on tiptoes.

"Git! Ya hear?"

Scott puffed and his cheeks expanded. Sounds flew out of his mouth. His eyes began to cross.

The man watched, eyes widening, as the boy continued to strain.

Finally, a smile cracked the weathered face - and became a grin, which exploded into deep laughter

When the man stopped, he saw the tiny hand outstretched. "You are one persistent cuss," he laughed. "Come over here."

Scott approached slowly - so close he could smell the ugly odors. He wrinkled his nose. The man continued chuckling. "This here," he said. "is all I got." And he put the change into the tiny palm.

Then the man struggled to his feet. "Well," he said, "I guess when you hit the bottom, it's time to start back up again. I think I'll go to the Mission and have a shower and a cot."

The man shuffled away, still smiling.

Sister Magdalena Murphy stared open mouthed at the offering. Her pale, freckled, angelic face expressed surprise, and she made a careful sign of the cross before speaking. "Scott

Dunlon," she said in her thickest Irish brogue, "Now where did you come about finding that much money?"

"My talent, sister!"

She eyed him curiously. "And what talent might that be?"

Scott smiled crookedly. "I can whistle. It makes people laugh."

Sister frowned. "Whistle up a laugh, can you? Sure, and that is a mighty talent God has given you." She eyed the stack of money. "But this is almost a hundred dollars, child. You whistled up that much in a day?"

Scott smiled. "Yes, sister."

"Lord Almighty! I guess I should be taking you to see Father."

Scott had never been in the old brick building before. He gaped at the dark wood paneling, the walls covered with religious paintings and photographs, and the huge wood crucifix mounted over the door.

"This is the Rectory, Scott. It's where Father Ryan lives."

Scott nodded as he admired the colored reflections that streamed into the entry hall from the stained glass window.

Sister led him to a small room off the entry. "Father Ryan?" she said quietly. "I brought you a visitor."

Sister motioned Scott into the room. Seated across the room behind a thick wooden desk, Father Ryan looked unhappy. "I haven't much time, Sister. The Bandinis will be here in ten minutes."

Sister Magdalena stared at the priest for a long time. "Ohhhhh."

The priest nodded.

Sister put Scott's money on the desk in front of the priest. "Father," she said. "Young Mister Dunloy here collected this money for the poor."

The priest eyed the pile. "Praise the Lord, Scott! How many months did it take to save this much money?"

"One day, Father."

The priest sat back in his chair and stared at the boy. "A single day?"

"Yes, Father."

Father Ryan waited several seconds, and when he continued, his voice was gentle. "Have you had your First Communion yet, Scott?"

"Next month, Father."

"Well, you know the difference between right and wrong?"

Scott nodded quickly. "Sure, Father!"

"And do you know about sins?"

Scott hesitated. "Some sins, father, but not all."

"Of course," the priest laughed. "Like lies - and stealing?"

"Oh, sure!"

"Good boy! Now, tell me how you got this much money."

"Whistling."

The priest eyed the boy. "Whistling? You mean..." The priest blew several weak notes.

Scott smiled. "Yes, Father. Whistling!"

'And people gave you money to whistle?"

Scott shook his head. "No, Father."

"What then?"

"My whistling made them laugh. They gave me money for that.""

Father Ryan eyed the nun, who shrugged.

"I'll show you, Father!"

The priest chuckled, but sounds in the hallway interrupted him. Footsteps. His face sagged, and he sighed deeply. "I am sorry, my son, but I have a very important meeting now. I want to talk to you tomorrow. And bring your mother."

"But I want to show you."

Father used the soft voice again. 'Tomorrow, child."

As Sister Magdalena ushered Scott from the office, they passed a family waiting in the hallway. Scott stopped.

A husband and wife pressed close together against the near wall. The man stared across the hall at a young girl. The wife stared at the floor and did not look up.

The girl had been crying. As Scott watched, she pressed a handkerchief to her eyes and glanced at him.

Scott approached the girl. "I'll sell you a smile."

The girl looked at him, knitted her brows, then burst into tears.

"I'll give you a smile for free."

She turned away – sobbing more deeply.

Sister Magdalena took Scott by the arm. "Come along, Scott. It's time to go."

Scott watched the girl over his shoulder until he has passed outside. On the sidewalk, he turned to Sister. "That girl needs me, Sister."

"Sure, and she could use more than that, poor thing."

"Let me go back and whistle for her!"

Sister sighed. "Not today, Scott. There may be some things even a whistle can't help."

Sister escorted Scott to his house. Scott waited until Sister turned the corner toward the convent, then he came back outside - and ran.

He did not stop until he neared the rectory.

Carefully, quietly, he opened the door.

He could hear voices inside Father Ryan's office.

A man's angry voice. "I'm sorry, Father, but I can't let her do it!"

A woman's sob. "It would ruin her life."

After a moment, Father Ryan's soft appeal. "You must understand. There is no other way."

"Then to hell with you!" The man shouted.

Scott gasped. He had never heard anyone talk to a priest this way before.

The woman's sob came louder. "Mother of God! She can't, Father! We can't!"

Scott pushed the heavy door. It opened soundlessly.

"I am truly sorry, Mrs. Bandini," Father Ryan said, his voice almost breaking into tears. "I will pray for you, and for Maria."

Scott walked quietly to Father's desk, then turned to face the Bandinis.

"Scott?" Father began. "What are you doing here?"

Scott didn't answer. Instead, he stood on tiptoes, puffed his cheeks, and blew. No sound except rushing air escaped his mouth.

"Oh, no!" he squealed. "Not now!"

He blew again. Still, no whistle sounded.

Tears suddenly fell down his small cheeks. He turned to Father Ryan and sobbed. "My gift away, Father. It's gone!"

Father, confused for a moment, smiled. "No, Scott. Jesus never takes away his gifts."

Scott took another breath.

The Bandinis eyed Scott skeptically. "What's this about, Father?" the man asked.

Father Ryan didn't answer.

Scott puffed. His eyes crossed. And the sound came. A squeak – a squeal – a Whistle! The sound was pure and perfect. Scott blew harder and the note resounded.

When Scott turned, Father Ryan was crying. "That was the most beautiful whistle I have ever heard. You are truly gifted!"

Mrs. Bandini stared at her lap and wept. Mr. Bandini wiped his eyes slowly.

Maria stared at the boy for an instant, burst into laughter, and then announced, "I'm keeping the baby!"

"Bless you child!" Father exclaimed.

"What did you say?" her father asked.

Maria looked at her parents. "I'm keeping the baby!"

"Oh, Maria! You can't!"

"I am!"

The mother spoke. "But what about school? Your friends?"

Maria laughed. "I'll work it out."

She pointed to Scott as she patted her middle. "He has a gift, and so do I."

It was Scott's turn to laugh.

ACT OF HONOR

"How many bodies, Chief?"

Master Chief Michael J. Hallahan studied the young officer for more than five seconds before handing over the photographs. "Twenty-three, sir!"

Ensign Donald Rockwell stared at the grainy images, then gasped, and his pale baby-face reddened. When he spoke, his voice cracked. "Twenty-three? All in one spot?"

"Well, sir, all within a fifty-foot radius."

"And all decomposed?"

"Yes, sir. Some clothing. Mostly bone."

Rockwell looked closer. "And all weighted down?"

"With chain, sir – heavy-duty."

Rockwell shivered. "Can we bring them up?"

"They're at 200 feet. It would take a little effort, but, yes, sir!"

Ensign Rockwell nodded. "Okay, Master Chief. I'll go topside and notify the skipper." He turned toward the water-tight door that served the dive locker.

"One more thing, Ensign."

Rockwell stopped, then turned slowly.

Master Chief Hallahan spoke. "I think they were Americans!"

More than fifty people crowded the Helo deck. All doors had been locked and enlisted guards stood outside. The skipper, Commander Gina E. 'Seabat' Wood, approached a podium. A seal with the ship's plaque was centered on the front, facing the officers. Bold raised letters above the seal read 'USS C. BURLINGAME' 'DDG 1971'.

Wood ran a hand through her short blonde hair and stared stony-faced at the crew before beginning. Her striking blue eyes reflected the harsh lighting. "Gentlemen. This briefing is classified as 'Secret'."

Several of the officers started a protest, but Wood raised her hands. "Wait!" she commanded. "I know some of you are not cleared that high, but I believe this is an extraordinary circumstance."

Commander Wood paused before continuing.

"Two days ago, Master Chief Hallahan discovered and photographed twenty-three bodies during a routine maintenance dive to repair a SOSUS buoy. What they were doing on the bottom of the South China Sea is anyone's guess." She paused. "We requested permission to bring them up."

Wood paused. "That permission has been denied!"

The audience murmured loudly. Wood held up her hands again. "Those are our orders! CINCPAC says the bodies are probably Japanese from the Second World War, and the Japanese government wants them to stay where they are. So we've been instructed to stick to our business and let the dead lie."

Master Chief Hallahan rose. Fluorescent lights glinted off his shaved and polished head. He spoke in a hard tone. "Ma'am! Then why the Secret hooey?"

Wood waited before answering. "I'm not sure, Master Chief. CINCPAC said the State Department ordered a security clampdown."

Hallahan smiled. "Well, It's not gonna work, skipper."

"Why?"

Ensign Rockwell stood. "Ma'am, the photos went electronically to Pearl Harbor yesterday."

Wood's voice became louder. "Under whose authority?"

Rockwell turned red but remained quiet.

Another officer stood. Tall, pencil thin, dark haired, and intense, Lieutenant Jack Conrad spoke. "Ma'am, I sent the photos!"

"What gave you the idea you could do that without permission, Doctor Conrad?"

"There were no orders to the contrary. Besides, it's my job!"

"How do you figure?"

"Sir! We discovered bodies. We had evidence of foul play. And those bodies might have been American." He paused. "As Ship's Physician, it was my duty to investigate. I sent the photos to Pearl for forensic review."

"You should have asked, Lieutenant."

"With all due respect, ma'am, that's not the way the Manual reads."

"The Manual be damned, Lieutenant! We have our orders!"

"Those orders are immoral, sir!"

"What?"

"Sir," Conrad said quickly. "I have reason to believe those bodies are American, and if they are, it's our honor-bound duty to bring them home."

"What is the basis for that presumption, Doctor?"

"This, sir!" It was Hallahan who spoke. He reached into his pocket and removed a small object. Striding smartly, he brought the object to the skipper.

Wood examined it closely. "Jesus, Chief! It's an Academy ring!"

"Look closer, ma'am!"

Wood turned the ring. Her face paled. "Oh, my God! Class of 67!"

"Japanese from World War Two!" Master Chief Hallahan bellowed. "What a crock of bullshit! CINCPAC knows exactly what we've found!"

"These are Americans, Commander," Doctor Conrad said. "Request permission to bring them home."

Still staring at the ring, Wood spoke quietly. "We have our orders."

"Orders, Skipper?!" the Master Chief yelled. "These are shipmates! We have a duty to them and their families."

"But – two hundred miles from nowhere in the middle of the South China Sea?"

Hallahan spoke again. "Not from 'nowhere', sir!"

Commander Wood stared at the rugged Master Chief for a long moment. "What do you mean, Master Chief?"

"We're two hundred miles from the mouth of Hanoi harbor. I, for one, think that's significant."

Doctor Christina Goto put down the microphone and studied the photo for the thousandth time. Standing, she walked to the window of her office in the Honolulu Medical Center overlooked the edge of the Haliakala Crater. The reflection showed a thin woman with soft, Japanese-American features and a youthful face that didn't quite match the Captain's eagle on the collar of her uniform blouse.

Someone knocked, then entered the office. She turned.

Three men in civilian coats and ties rushed in. One went immediately to her computer. Another went to her desk and began rifling papers. The third, a stocky man with a florid complexion, approached her.

"Is this a robbery?" she asked calmly.

The leader snickered as he pulled out a wallet. Identification flashed in front of her face. "Agent Boteller. NSA, Doctor. My associates are Agents Foley and Swetland. We need to get every copy of those photos you received form the Burlingame. Plus any notes and records of communication."

"Excuse me," she replied. "But what is your name, please?"

Boteller continued. "Look, Doc! We can do this the easy way or the hard way. Your choice."

"What's the hard way?"

His face reddened. "The hard way is I haul you off to the Brig."

"On what charge?"

"Interfering with a Security investigation for starters."

Doctor Goto laughed. "That's a lie and you know it."

The man reached behind him a pulled out a set of handcuffs. "Okay! The hard way it is!"

"Found it!" The operative by the computers shouted. "I erased the file!"

"All of it? Plus reference files?"

He held up a thumbdrive. "I used the 'scrubber'."

Boteller addressed the other man. "Any paperwork?"

"Yes, sir! The photos and some notes."

"Bring it all!"

"Aye, aye, sir!"

The Lead Agent stared at Doctor Goto and smirked. "Captain Goto! Under the power of the National Security Act of 1948, I hereby restrict you from further work on the Burlingame photos or in any manner to continue with research or to discuss this issue with any other person. Any violation will be regarded as a breach of National Security and you will be treated accordingly, including Courts Martial, prison, and potential loss of pay and benefits."

With that, the three men departed.

"Once the door was closed, Goto laughed. "Eat shit, spook boy!"

"What are you doing, Master Chief?"

Hallahan stared hard at Ensign Rockwell. "Go away, Ensign!"

"Hey!" Rockwell laughed. "You can't talk to an officer that way."

Hallahan smiled. "I talked to your daddy that way when he was an Ensign. It worked once, I recon it'll work again."

Rockwell examined the equipment. "You're gonna check that SOSUS buoy, right?"

"Sure thing!"

"And you need a heavy-duty welding rig?"

Hallahan smiled. "I might have to fix something."

"You wouldn't be thinking about cutting something – like heavy chain?'

"Well, if it was in the way…"

Rockwell frowned. "Master Chief! You know the orders."

"Yes, sir!"

The two men stared at each other for a long time. Rockwell sighed. "My daddy used to talk about you a lot. He said you were a phenom – and a terrific pain in the ass." He chuckled. "But he also said that I should trust your instincts. So, I think I'll go up to the Officer's Mess and have a cup of coffee while you're getting ready. I'll probably be back once you're underwater."

Hallahan nodded, and a slight smile lit his rugged features.

The bridge of the USS Burlingame was quiet when the radioman entered. "Skipper," he said. "I have Top Secret message traffic from Pearl."

Commander Wood took the sealed envelope and retired to her cabin.

When she returned a minute later, Ensign Rockwell waited for her.

"How soon will the SOSUS work be finished, Ensign?"

"Hard to say, ma'am. Couple hours. Couple days. Depends on what the Master Chief finds."

"We may need to get underway in a few hours. Call the Master Chief and tell him to get ready to come up."

"What's the problem, ma'am?"

Wood glared Rockwell into silence.

After Rockwell departed, Commander Wood motioned to the Executive Officer. "Please join me on the starboard wing, Commander."

Lieutenant Commander Thomas Gross followed Commander Wood out onto the starboard side wing. "Get inside, lookout!" Wood snapped. "And dog the hatch!"

The lookout retreated. The watertight door clanged shut behind them. Wood watched until the hatch was locked down.

"What's up, skipper?"

"Trouble!"

Gross waited. He watched the Commander's face.

Wood stared at the message. "The Chinese Navy is headed this way."

"Excuse me, ma'am?"

She nodded. "You heard me right. Two small destroyers and a gunboat. With more on the way."

"But why?"

"No idea. The Chinese claim a missile exercise of some kind. The CINCPAC message was cryptic. Told me to get the work done fast, then get out of here."

"Missiles? What kind?"

"It's not in the Briefing Book," she replied. "CINCPAC has diverted the SCHAUFELBERGER this way, but they're more than 200 miles east. The Chinese ships should arrive within 4 hours."

"Shit! What the hell do they want?"

Wood laughed harshly. "You know that as well as I do, Commander Gross."

"The bodies?"

"Damn right!"

"But who told them?"

Wood laughed again. "Who do you think?"

"Bastards! So we're supposed to move aside and let the Vietnamese 'Exercise' destroy the evidence?"

"That's my guess."

Gross hesitated. "I guess we better get Hallahan out of the water."

Wood didn't answer.

"I don't care about security, Admiral! And you shouldn't either."

Captain Goto sat in the chair opposite the Admiral's huge oak desk. "They're following me, you know!"

"Who?"

"NSA. They've been watching my quarters and following me to the Hospital. I suspect they have a tap on my phone and my E-Mail."

Admiral Biff Hergenroeder grunted, and his jaw muscles started working as a feverish pace. "And what am I supposed to do?"

"I need to talk to you in private, and I need military security around."

"Marines?"

"You bet!"

Admiral Hergenroeder punched the intercom button. "Lieutenant Murphy. Get a Security Detachment here to my office. ASAP! Code Blue!"

"Armed, sir?"

"That is what Code Blue means, does it not?"

"Aye, aye, sir!"

The Admiral placed two overly large hands on the desk. "All right Goto. Talk! But it better be good."

Captain Goto stood. "Turn your head, Admiral!"

"What? Why?"

She laughed. "So I can get to what I need to show you."

Admiral Hergenroeder laughed, then spun around.

Less than a minute later, Captain Goto announced. "Ready, sir!"

Goto had spread a series of photographs on the small circular table. "Over here, Admiral."

The Admiral approached the table. "I knew it. The China Sea bodies!"

"Yes, Admiral," she replied. "The China Sea bodies."

He laughed. "It's a few poor Japanese sailors, Captain. I've seen the reports."

"The reports are a lie, sir! The bodies are American POWs left behind after the war in Vietnam. They were killed recently – within three years - and dumped at sea to hide all trace of it."

"Three years? Impossible!"

"No sir!" she answered. "The evidence is clear. And not only were they dumped recently, but they were alive shortly before they hit the water."

Admiral Hergenroeder's face underwent a change. His eyes widened, and his face became red. Christine watched the vein in his temple pulsing.

"Alive?"

"Yes, sir!"

"You have proof?"

"Nearly incontrovertible! There's ample evidence in the photographs of tooth wear, recent injuries, arthritis. Five minutes with the remains will prove it."

"Dear God! Do you know what this means?"

"I don't want to imagine."

Shouting in the anteroom disturbed them. "What the hell!" the Admiral shouted. He approached the door.

"Careful, Admiral!"

"The hell you say!" Hergenroeder flung open the door.

Outside in the anteroom, Marine guards tussled with several men in civilian clothes. One guard had a bead on the group with his M16.

"What's going on here?" The Admiral bellowed.

One of the men spoke as he flashed credentials. "Admiral Hergenroeder. I'm Lead Agent Joe Boteller with NSA. We have reason to believe that Captain Christina Goto is a high-risk security leak. We are here to arrest her in the name of the Attorney General of the United States."

"Captain Goto is in my office!"

The Lead Agent smiled. "Then if you'll just hand her over, we'll be on our way."

The Admiral nodded to the Marine Lieutenant on duty. "Lieutenant Doyle, unholster your weapon and escort this gentleman inside."

The Lead Agent eyed the Admiral, then turned to one of the other Agents. "Stevens! Get back to the car and radio in. Tell them we may need back-up."

"Corporal!" The Admiral addressed the Marine with the aimed weapon.

"Yes, sir!"

"Until I get to the bottom of this, none of these gentlemen are to leave this office or communicate in any way with the outside. Call the Barracks and get a Reaction force over here. Code Blue." He stared at the Lead Agent. "And Corporal! If one of these gentlemen tries anything provocative – shoot 'em!"

The Lead Agent's face went white. "Admiral!"

"Get your ass in my office. Now!"

"Lieutenant! Cover him!"

"Aye aye, sir!"

"Skipper! Master Chief Hallahan is aboard. He wants to talk to you immediately!"

"Get him up here!"

"He says you need to come down there."

Commander Wood nodded, then followed the messenger down the ladder.

The Dive Locker was strangely quiet when she entered. Master Chief Hallahan had the hard cover off and was unsuiting. Crewmen surrounded him.

"What is so important, Master Chief, that I had to come down here?"

Hallahan's face was flushed and his eyes were watery. He sniffed as he reached a hand toward the Skipper. A thin metal chain dangled from his fingers, at the end of which swung two thin metal wafers.

"Dog Tags?" Wood asked.

"Yes, ma'am! Vietnam Era!"

Commander Wood accepted the gift gently. "Down there?"

Hallahan nodded.

"How many?"

His rugged face reddened. "Too f-ing many!!!" Hallahan screamed. "They are Americans! Dumped here because they were in the way of political progress!"

"You don't know that, Master Chief."

A tear rushed down Hallahan's face. "I do know that I had Riverine friends go missing in that stinking war who never turned up again. These could be my shipmates."

"What else did you find?"

"Lots of miscellaneous items that could only be American."

"But why here?"

"Why not? What are the chances anyone would ever find them this far at sea? Ashore, and maybe somebody digs 'em up or talks too much."

Staring hard at the dogtags, Commander Wood sighed and her features hardened. "How long to recover the bodies, Master Chief.?"

"Six. Maybe eight hours."

"We may not have that kind of time. It appears some Chinese ships are headed this way and CINCPAC asked us to depart the area immediately."

"Tell CINCPAC what we've found. I know Admiral Hergenroeder personally. He's a firebrand!"

Commander Wood had not looked up. She slipped the dogtags over her head. "Recover the bodies!" She rushed from the room.

"This skull belongs to Lieutenant Richard Hornmel, USN. Shot down over Hanoi in 1969."

"That's Bullshit!" the Agent screamed.

The Admiral addressed Captain Goto. "How do you know that?"

She smiled. "See the teeth. Look at the dental pattern. Here's the last Dental X-Ray given to the Captain. Except for a few missing teeth that I can attribute to poor nutrition and old age, It's an exact match."

"You're wrong!" The Agent shouted. "You will all lose your careers for this!"

Admiral Hergenroeder turned to the NSA Agent. His eyes were wild. "I am a Vice Admiral. I've been in the Navy since 1967. My career is almost over." He pointed a finger. "If what I am seeing here is real, and if I think for a second that you are part of a coverup to hide that fact that American military personnel have been prisoner all this time. And if you, sir, are supporting that lie, I will take the good Lieutenant's weapon and shoot you dead!" His voice lowered and the next word he spoke slowly. "Do – you - understand - me?"

The Agent nodded.

The intercom buzzed. "Admiral," the voice said, "we have a Ship-to-Shore voice message coming in on a secured channel."

"I'm in an important conference!"

"Sir! This is from the Burlingame. The Skipper needs to talk to you. She says it's a matter of National Security."

The Admiral went to the secured phone and lifted the receiver. "CINCPAC! This is Admiral Hergenroeder!"

"Admiral, this is Commander Wood and Master Chief Hallahan. We have a grave situation developing here."

"I thought I ordered you to finish the repairs, then get underway."

"Sir! I'm not sure that would be prudent. We have convincing evidence that the bodies below us are U. S. POWS"

Hergenroeder grunted. "What's your status, Commander?"

"We are on station. Diving has ceased. Chinese ships are two hours away!"

Hergenroeder looked hard at the Agent. "Anything you need to tell me, Mister?"

The Agent shook his head. "Get that ship out of there. You'll create an International Incident. The President's orders!"

Hergenroeder laughed. "Yeah? I'm betting those orders don't come from the White House. So, until the President calls me, I'm still in charge here." He spoke into the phone. "Can you recover the bodies, Commander?"

"Yes, sir! But it should take a while."

"Do it!"

"And what about the Chinese?"

"Radio them! Tell them you are conducting underwater repairs and tell then to stand down."

"And if they don't?"

"Protect your ship and crew, Commander!"

"Can I get some air support?"

"I'll do my best, but I think you're going to be mostly on your own."

"Aye, aye, Sir!"

Hergenroeder hung up the phone, then turned to the Marine. "Lieutenant. Take these intruders to the Brig! Strip them! Search them for contraband. Take their statements."

"Just a minute!" the Agent yelled. "I demand that I be able to contact Washington!"

Admiral Hergenroeder grinned. "You will, Mister Agent Boteller. In about eight hours!" He waved toward the door. "Get these cockroaches out of my sight."

"Yes, sir!!!"

The Admiral followed them to the door. "And no need to be gentle, Lieutenant!"

"Understand, sir!"

Admiral Hergenroeder went to his desk and sat. "You better get along, Captain."

"Aye, sir. What about you?"

He sighed. "I'm going to stay here and listen in on the situation. Then I have a resignation letter to write."

Commander Wood ran onto the Bridge. Before the messenger could say a word she was shouting. "Prepare for Dive Operations."

Lieutenant Commander Gross nodded slowly. "We're staying, Ma'am?"

"Yes! And let's take the ship to General Quarters! Arm the missiles and free the batteries."

Gross almost stumbled. "We're gonna fight?"

"If we have to? Damn right we are! It looks like the war that never ended is coming to a close today, gentlemen. Look sharp!"

The Alarm sounded, drowning out conversation. The sounds of hundreds of crew hurrying to their stations filled the ship. Within seconds, the XO reported. "The ship is now at General Quarters, Skipper."

Wood looked at her watch and smiled. "That fast? Well, XO, that may be a new Navy record."

Gross smiled sheepishly. "I told the Department Heads you sort of might do something like this."

Wood laughed as a voice came over the loud speaker. "Bridge, this is Weapons. All weapons free, Skipper! Where do you want 'em?"

"Target the three ships coming over the horizon! Cannon and missiles. Nothing stealth! I want the bastards to know they're about to die!"

On the forward section of the ship turrets turned westward. In seconds the voice sounded again. "We have a lock on all three targets, ma'am!"

A new voice sounded. "Bridge, this is CIC. "They're pinging back! They have targeted us!"

"Ready the Phalanx, Weaps! It's a battle of nerves from here on."

Rockwell's voice echoes throughout the bridge. "Hallahan is on the bottom!"

Commander Wood nodded. "Roger that!"

"The Chinese are still coming!"

"Let's let 'em know we mean business. Weaps! Fire a round 100 yards forward of the lead ship's bow!"

"Aye aye!"

The ship rocked as the 54 caliber gun fired. In the distance a splash erupted.

"Still coming, Skipper!"

"Fire again! Fifty yards this time!"

Another round went off.

Rockwell's voice sounded again. "Hallahan says the first body is recovered!"

"Tell the Master Chief, great work!"

"Still coming, skipper!"

Wood turned to the XO. "I have fired over their bow twice. I'm tired of wasting Government money on bullets. Get me on the horn to the lead ship!"

"Do you speak their lingo?"

"How much you want to bet they speak ours?"

Gross switched on the ship's radio and spoke. "Chinese ships, this is USS Burlingame. Do you read, over."

"American ship! American ship! Cease fire and depart the area!"

Wood grabbed the microphone. "Sorry, but we've got men in the water."

"You must leave. We are conducting an exercise and may accidentally injure your crew."

"Harm anyone and I'll send you to the bottom!"

"You must depart!"

"It's too late!"

"What do you mean?"

"We have the bodies."

"What bodies?"

"It's all over! And I am tired of play acting. Stand down or be ready to fight!"

Silence followed. The ships continued their approach. Wood nodded to the XO. "Keep the mike open. I want them to know what we're doing." She pressed the intercom button and spoke loudly. "I want the first missile dead center on the Captain's chair of the lead ship, Weaps. Can you do that? Stand by!"

"Roger, Skipper. Splash one chair!"

"Ready Missiles! On my command! Ten…Nine…Eight…!"

"They're stopped pinging. They're turning, ma'am!" the XO yelled.

"Track 'em until they're out of range!"

"Roger that!"

Commander Wood turned to Lieutenant Commander Gross. "Tell Hallahan he's got some extra time, but not to dawdle. Then call Admiral Hergenroeder and tell him all's well. I'm driving the boat straight back to Pearl and I'll have some presents for the American people when I arrive."

PENANCE

Archbishop Murphy must have heard about my computer skills. Even though I was fresh from the St. Mary's Seminary, he had asked that I help in the Baltimore Archdiocese before I went to my assigned Parish. Mostly it was database work – hardly worthy of my undergrad Computer Science and Mathematics degrees, but, when the Archbishop calls, we neophyte Priests must answer – and gladly.

But the Archbishop had also posed a question that had had me baffled for several days. How to determine the number of Baltimore Catholics that had fallen away from the Church – without spending a small fortune. It was an exercise in mathematics and that I hadn't been able to get my hands around, and he wanted an answer by week's end.

So the stage was set. It was Monday afternoon and I sat huddled at a small desk in the corner of a room normally reserved for mail sorting. I had just finished collating the Saint Catherine's data and was reading a text on statistical sampling when Archbishop Murphy burst into the room. Having just left a meeting with the Knights of Columbus, he was in his full regalia – red, black, and purple. All that was lacking was his Bishop's crook. His portly frame jiggled as he hurried to the front of my desk.

"Father Matchuk!" he yelled. "Get your coat and come with me!"

I must have looked confused. He waved his arms frantically. "Hurry, Father. There's no time to waste."

As I struggled my black jacket over my cassock, I imagined all sorts of calamities, catastrophes, and dire circumstances. "Should I bring the Holy Chrisms?" I asked.

He stopped, then stared at me like I was crazy. "What? No!" He shook his head. "This is not a physical or clerical disaster."

"What is it, then, Your Eminence?" I asked.

"God help us!" he yelled. "But Father Wyatt is loose!"

I started to ask the obvious questions, but the Archbishop grabbed my arm and pulled. "No time for talk, Father. You have a sports car, don't you?"

"Yes, Your Eminence," I replied. I felt myself redden. "A Corvette. Convertible. I've had it for a number of years."

"That'll do. You drive. Take us to the corner of Pratt and Light Streets. Fast!"

Archbishop Murphy rested a Rosary on his ample belly and prayed Hail Marys the entire twenty blocks. I hadn't learned the protocol for interrupting an Archbishop in prayer, so I stayed quiet. But, I was suitably intrigued.

As we approached the busy intersection, I realized we had a difficulty. "Where do we park, your Eminence?"

He looked up from his beads. "Anywhere," he answered.

"There are no spots on the street. Should I find a garage?"

"No, no," he stammered. "Stop here. Hurry!"

"But……"

"Do it Father!"

I stopped the car at the curb, set the brake, snapped on the emergency blinkers, and got out. The driver of the car behind leaned out of his window. "Hey!" he yelled. Then he saw my collar. "Oh, sorry, Father."

I smiled and shrugged as he put on his blinker to get around us.

If it hadn't been for the low-slung nature of the Vet, Archbishop Murphy wouldn't have waited for me. When I came around to the passenger side, I found him, door open, struggling to get out. His face was flushed and his whispy hair disheveled. I offered a hand.

I must have been smiling. I mean, it was a comical sight.

He didn't see the humor. "Father Matchuk, please!" he said sternly. "I seem to be wedged into place. And there's no time for any of this. Help me!"

I am a fairly strong man, but it took several long seconds to extricate Archbishop Murphy. While we struggled, I noted that passing motorists fell into two distinct camps. Those who were amused with our predicament, and those who were angry that we had slowed their progress. Arbitrarily, I decided that first group must have been Catholic, and the second - Calvinists.

Once free of the seat, Archbishop Murphy stared at the Corvette with distaste. Then he surveyed the surroundings and sighed. "We've lost him for sure," he said.

"Father Wyatt?" I asked.

"Of course, Father Wyatt!" he snapped.

A Patrol car pulled behind us, lights flashing.

"Baltimore's finest," Archbishop Murphy muttered. "Late as usual."

I could see the driver, a burly, florid-faced, giant, staring at us as he spoke into his radio. His partner, a young, thin, black man, exited, then, eyeing us suspiciously, began to direct traffic.

As the driver approached, the Archbishop stepped in front of me and stared at the policeman's namebadge. "I'm glad you are here, Officer Kunkowski. I'm Archbishop Murphy. We are responding to an emergency."

The policeman nodded. "How can I help?"

Archbishop Murphy grabbed my arm and led me past the patrol car. "Oh, you can't help," he answered. "You see, we are here to find a runaway Priest. It's very delicate."

"Runaway?" The Officer and I said it simultaneously. Kunkowski raised both eyebrows, and we stared at each other for several seconds. I almost called 'Jinx'.

"No time to explain," the Archbishop said. "Call Commissioner Daly! Tell him Father Wyatt is loose. He'll understand." He stopped. "Oh." He pointed at my car. "And please see that Father's sardine can remains safe."

I looked backward and shrugged at the policemen as the Archbishop spoke distractedly. "We'll have to try the taverns first, I suppose."

I didn't ask why.

The establishment was named, *Oriole Inn*. The bar and all the tables were packed with afternoon patrons. The presence of a Priest and an elderly Bishop standing just inside the doorway attracted some small attention. Archbishop Murphy moaned, since being somewhat limited in stature, he could not see over the crowd. He tried to stand on tiptoe. "This is not going to be easy. I swear he does it on purpose."

"Who? Father Wyatt?" I asked.

Judging by his look, I began to wonder if the Archbishop considered me dim witted. "Of course, Father Wyatt!" he stammered. "It's just like him."

"Archbishop," I whispered. "I could help if I knew what to look for."

He paused, stared up at me, then took a deep breath. "Father Wyatt – Monsignor Wyatt, really - was 82 on his last birthday. He is six feet tall, bald, and uses a walker – that is when he's not running away from the Archdiocese Retirement Home."

It started to fall into place. I scanned the crowd. "No one like that is here, your Eminence."

"Hurry!" he said. "Let's try the next place."

As we hustled along the sidewalk, mostly against the flow of human traffic, I spoke, foolishly thinking I had the situation figured out. "Has he been missing long? Are you concerned for father's safety?"

"It's not his safety I'm concerned about!" Archbishop Murphy said. "It's ours."

All the pieces fell out of place. "I'm sorry, your Eminence. I don't understand."

He stopped, looked around at the people, then pulled me against the side of a building. Soto voce, he said. "Father Wyatt was the Archdiocese *Father Confessor* for twenty-five years. He retired ten years ago. Now seems to be getting a little confused."

"Dementia?" I asked.

"God forgive me, if only it were that simple." He paused. "Father Wyatt, the quietest man you would ever know, has developed a sudden need for attention. He likes to tell stories to attractive young ladies."

"There was a time when I did the same thing, your Eminence. He's 82 and senile. He must be harmless."

Archbishop Murphy shook his head. "He's heard the confessions of every local Catholic politician in the last forty years. And now he wants to share them."

"Oh, my God!"

"Yes," the Archbishop echoed. "Oh, my God!" He paused. "And do you know the worse part?"

I shook my head.

"We can't even know if the things he says are true."

The trail warmed at the next tavern. A group of three well-dressed young women passed us at the door, then huddled into a tight group and tittered as they walked away.

"Wait!" Archbishop Murphy commanded.

One of them, an overly thin blonde, with near-elfin features, must have been Catholic. She stopped short, then immediately looked down at the sidewalk. The others stared at her, then paused.

We approached.

"You've been talking to Father Wyatt, I suppose?" he asked.

The blonde answered. " 'Father' Wyatt?"

"Yes, yes! An elderly man. Bald. Garrulous."

"He was a priest?" One of the companions, a tall, overly-proportioned brunette, asked. "Oh my God!"

Murphy addressed the young blonde. "You're a Catholic?"

"Yes, Father..." she stammered. "I mean, Bishop…Your Eminence…"

"That old man was a Priest?" the brunette asked again.

Murphy ignored her. He addressed the blonde. "What's your name, child?"

"Kara, sir! Kara Glowacki."

"Did Father Wyatt say where he was headed, Kara?"

"Let him have his fun!" the brunette interrupted.

The other girl was a 'libber' from what I could see. She had a hard, arrogant look on her face. "Don't tell him, Kara!" she demanded.

Archbishop Murphy shook his head, then addressed the women. "I wonder if you would humor me and not speak to anyone about what Father Wyatt might have shared with you." He paused. "At one time he was the best Priest in Baltimore. A shining example to Catholics and non-Catholics alike."

The brunette gave a suggestive wiggle, then laughed. "Some example."

"Hey!" I interrupted. "Show some respect!" This got their attention. – and Archbishop Murphy's. I softened my next words. "Father's gotten senile. He doesn't realize what he's doing or saying. We're trying to get him back to a safe place."

Kara looked at her companions, then stared at the Archbishop, her face reddening. "The *Two O'Clock Club*," she answered. The other girls giggled.

"A strip joint?" I asked.

Kara nodded. "That's what he said. It's just two blocks away, around the corner on Saratoga Street."

"Let's go along," the brunette suggested. "This could be fun."

"No!" said Kara. "I couldn't."

"Not me," the other answered. "Too sexist."

I never told anyone – except in Confession – that I had been to the *Two O'Clock Club* once in my Senior year at Johns Hopkins. I was a real nerd at the time, solely interested in Computer things, and I woke up one morning two weeks before graduation realizing that I had never experienced anything, and I vowed to end that deficiency. That evening I went alone to downtown Baltimore to visit the notorious *Two O'Clock Club*. It was everything I had imagined – and less. And here it was in front of me again.

I hadn't seen it in the daylight. It was awful. Rundown. Seedy. Pagan. Lurid posters of overdeveloped women, half-naked and caked in makeup and lip glosses, covered the front walls of the building. Archbishop Murphy purposefully ignored the advertisements and squinted at the barker, who stood out front calling to passers by.

The Archbishop's look must have seemed angry and intimidating. When the barker saw us, he stopped, then stiffened.

His expression tightened as he moved toward us, trying to block our view of the advertisements. "Welcome to the *Two O'Clock Club,* Fathers." He lowered his voice. "I can see by your garb and your demeanor that you are here on business, not pleasure, so let me be up front with you. We are a legitimate establishment. No touching. No back-room action. No hanky-panky. We don't want no trouble. We're a Baltimore landmark, and the girls are just making a living."

"Did an elderly man enter in the last half hour?" Archbishop Murphy blurted.

The barker laughed. "Most of the patrons are elderly, Father. And even they come and go quickly. That's the way it is in the business these days. Too much free love. Too many suggestive video games. And don't get me started about the Internet." He shook his head. "It's practically ruined us."

"Yes, yes!" Archbishop Murphy stammered, then looked at me, pleadingly.

"I'll handle this, your Eminence," I offered. "I know the drill."

The barker stared at me, wondering, I'm sure who this new animal was. A Priest who knew the routines of a strip club?

I pretended to be savvier than I was. I bulled my way past the barker and entered the dark foyer. "What about the Cover Charge?" the barker shouted.

"Deduct it from your next charitable contribution," The archbishop sputtered, then turned away from the building – most probably to avoid temptation.

Hard, pulsating music assaulted me as I entered. And lights, flashing in stroboscopic colors. And the smell of decades-old tobacco mixed with thick perfumes and desperate sweat. On stage a blonde woman, impossibly thin, decidedly unhappy, and gravitationally exempt, gyrated around a brass pole. It was unnerving. I prayed a Hail Mary before continuing into the gloom.

I saw him immediately – sitting at a booth near the entry, crooked fingers curled around a mixed drink. Two women, one blonde, one brunette, both tightly clothed, legs showing past mid-thigh, sat closely on either side, smoking and laughing. Father Wyatt said something. They laughed again.

He didn't notice me. His mind was elsewhere. As I approached, he started to take a drink - and saw me. His shoulders sagged. He put his glass carefully down and lowered his gaze to the glossy table.

The women noticed his change. The blonde looked up. "Oh," she said, then slid out of the booth and slipped away. The brunette followed suit. "Sorry, Father." She pulled at her skirt and stared at me as she left. The guilt in her demeanor was palpable.

I stopped. A Catholic? Working? In here?

Father Wyatt stared at me. His startlingly blue eyes reflected the surrounding chaos. He nodded.

"Father Wyatt?" I asked.

"Yes, Father," he said so quietly I could barely hear. "And who has found me?"

"I'm Father Matchuk. Fresh from Seminary and temporarily assigned to the Archdiocese."

He glanced past me toward the door, then smiled. When he spoke, it was in a loud, but humorous, tone. "What, no squad of police like the last time? Isn't the Archbishop afraid I will overpower you and run away?"

The music stopped and the stage show ground to a halt. Everyone, including the overdeveloped dancer, was watching us, waiting.

I chuckled. "No, Father. The Archbishop was happy enough just to find you so quickly." I gave a sweep of my hand. "Do you always attract so much attention?"

He looked around, then pointed to my cassock and laughed. "This time, I think it's you, Father."

He patted the seat next to him. "Please, sit down. Talk to me for a minute."

I slipped into the booth with my back to the dancer but when I looked up I saw that mirrors throughout the room reflected the stage image so that I could not avoid the flesh-trap. I closed my eyes and said another Hail Mary.

When I opened my eyes Father Wyatt was watching me curiously. Waiting.

"Tell me something, Father?" I asked.

He nodded.

"Why are you doing this?"

He stared hard at me. "The escaping? The bars? The young women?"

I shook my head. "You know what I really mean, Father."

He sighed, the nodded. "The answer is Penance."

Almost on cue, the music started up again and the brunette waitress approached us. She stared at Father Wyatt with near reverence. In this setting, it was eerie and I had instant chills. I shook my head. Father Wyatt smiled at her. "Jack Daniels, Barbara. Straight up," he ordered. "Water for me, please," I said.

I started to speak, but he placed a hand on my arm and squeezed. "I can explain it all," he said. I waited as he took a deep breath and closed his eyes.

"Confessions are my priestly specialty, Father," he began. "It didn't start out that way, of course. I managed two Parishes before coming to the Archdiocese. I offered a devout Mass and preached a very good homily. My parishioners appreciated me." He smiled. "And for some reason, I really brought them into the confessional. Some Saturdays I heard Confessions for three hours. Cleansing souls. Infusing the Holy Spirit. Forgiving sins.

"Somehow," he continued, "Old Bishop Doyle found out about my gift, and I became the Archdiocese Father Confessor."

"It's an awesome gift Christ has given Priests, Father Matchuk. The power to forgive sins or hold them bound."

He paused and his hand squeezed my arm with a power I would have thought impossible in a man his age. Then he jerked his head to indicate his surroundings. "There is so much sin, Father. And we Catholics don't really appreciate the harm it does. To us. To our families. To our neighbors."

He let go of my arm and sighed, and for the first time he seemed old.

Looking at the glossy table top, he whispered. "The Lord speaks to me, Father. He is a constant voice in my head. There's so much to do."

His gaze snapped upward and locked onto my face. I nearly drew away. I didn't like where he was heading. Reflexively, I withdrew my Rosary from my pocket and placed it on the table, careful not to let it go.

"Nobody believes in sin anymore," he continued. "Everyone thinks that they can lead whatever life they want, and so long as they are sorry at the instant when they pass on, God will forgive them and they get a free pass into Heaven – after a brief stop in Purgatory, of course – if they even believe in that."

"He will forgive them!" I answered a bit too loudly.

He chuckled. "Of course He will – if they are truly sorry. No one would consciously choose damnation if they understood it. But they don't, you see, and so many are going to hell by degrees, Father."

I started to protest, but he held up a wrinkled hand. He stared over my shoulder and smiled.

A nearby voice startled me. "God still forgives, Albert. All sins."

I looked up, as Archbishop Murphy settled into the booth next to me.

Father Wyatt shook his head and smiled at Archbishop Murphy. "I've become an expert on sins, haven't I, Michael? Remember the Garden? One simple rule – Don't eat from a single tree. Adam and Eve broke the rule - and death and disease and all the horrors of life entered the world. You can bet they were sorry then, but it was too late, wasn't it?"

Neither Archbishop Murphy nor I answered for nearly a minute. I didn't completely understand what he was saying, but the implications frightened me. "So," I finally said. "Why are you here?"

"I come to Satan's dens to scare them straight," he answered. "It's my gift."

"And why the 'Doddering Priest' act?" the Archbishop asked.

"To get their attention, Michael" he answered. "Satan has a strong hold. I have to be subtle. They'll listen to me if I play the old fool - but not if I preach."

"It's what God calls you to do?" I asked.

"I think He wants this to be my final Penance," he answered. He looked around. "Gather as many souls as I can and bring them back before they are lost – or I am dead."

Archbishop Murphy shook his head. "We put you in a nice home, Albert. You've been a good priest for fifty years. It's time to let the young guard take over."

The waitress approached again. Without a word, she slipped into the booth next to Father Wyatt and whispered into his ear. He nodded. Her whispering continued for more than a minute, punctuated occasionally by a nod from Father Wyatt. Finally he lifted a hand to her head, made a slow sign of the cross, then kissed her gently on the cheek. "Go with God,

Barbara." She smiled through huge tears. "Thank you, Father." Then she departed, stepping lightly through the gloom. Somehow I could tell this was her last night at *"The 2 O'Clock Club."*

We watched her leave, quiet, considering. I found myself praying the 'Act of Contrition'. Father Wyatt stared at the Archbishop. "I'm not ready to give this up, Michael" he said. "God calls me."

"It's just not safe, Father." Archbishop Murphy replied. "I can't agree."

"What if I were the escort?" I blurted.

They both stared at me, open-mouthed.

"What if I picked up Father Wyatt at the Retirement Home a couple days a week? Took him wherever he wanted to go – wherever he will do the most good. Then let him loose on the crowds. I could watch from the sidelines to make sure he was safe, and he could save souls."

Archbishop Murphy started to protest, but I interrupted. "And I could conduct random surveys of the people we meet. Gather data for the analysis." I paused. "I think I could get your answers faster this way, Your Eminence."

Father Wyatt perked up. "Mobility! Praise God!" He laughed. "At my age, it's the one thing I lack."

He paused. "But we'd need to move quickly, Father. Go where the need is." He chuckled. "You've got to be fast to stay ahead of the Devil."

"Fast?" I answered. "Not a problem!"

He looked at me quizzically.

"I drive a Corvette. The Devil will have trouble keeping up with us."

Archbishop Murphy watched the two of us for a moment, then chuckled. "I hope God forgives me, Albert."

We stared at the Archbishop.

He continued. "I think I just made a decision to let a senile old priest and a fresh-from-seminary sidekick loose on the poor people of Baltimore. Somehow it seems unfair for them."

Father Wyatt became serious. He raised his hand and made a sign-of-the-cross in the Archbishop's direction. "I forgive you, Archbishop. For your penance you'll have to deal with the consequences of that glorious decision."

AUTOMATIC TELLER

The machine churned and clicked. In the bottom tray, three twenty-dollar bills slid forward. She glanced from side-to-side – no one was nearby. Despite that, she snatched the money and stuffed it into her purse.

"That should be enough for dinner," she whispered.

She wiped the screen clean with a tissue and examined her appearance in the glass. She knew she wasn't much to look at. Stringy hair, the color of ripe acorns, cut short against the sides of her head. Brown eyes too dark to be interesting. Thin, nearly imaginary, lips. A sallow, blotchy, complexion. And worse yet, a figure so far past Rubenesque that it bordered on obesity. No, she decided, she wasn't much. And at thirty-three, the fact that she had attracted a man at all was incredible.

Looking at her watch, she sighed. "God, I hope he's not late."

DO YOU WANT TO MAKE ANOTHER TRANSACTION?

"No, thank you." She pushed the "NO" space on the computer screen and waited.

The machine emitted a different sound. The whirring took longer this time.

"Hurry please!" She said aloud. "I have an important appointment!"

The machine beeped, and a message appeared on the screen.

GOOD EVENING MISS WILSON.

Odd! She never remembered the Teller Machine greeting her by name. But, of course, the system must know who she was. Probably an improvement – trying to get more personal.

Addressing the Teller, she made a slight bow. "It's nice to be greeted." Then she glanced down to the bottom line, then spoke aloud. "Seventy-one hundred dollars and twenty-three cents!" She smiled. "That's quite a dowry!"

She was turning to go when the machine began clicking again. Curious, she waited. "Do you have something else for me?"

The sounds went on even longer than the first time. She had nearly decided to leave when another message appeared on the glass.

HE IS NOT FOR YOU, MISS WILSON. HAVE NOTHING FURTHER TO DO WITH HIM!

She nearly dropped the note. "Who?" She said aloud.

Another note.

PLEASE LISTEN TO ME. HE IS A PREDATOR!

Frowning, she examined the machine where it fastened to the wall of the bank. Nothing unusual.

She checked the time. "Five-thirty. Oh my God! I'll be late!"

She hurried to her Red Honda Civic, squeezed herself into the seat, and raced away.

"It is so nice to see you, Helen dear!" As he spoke, he raised her hand to his mouth and kissed it. The stiff hairs of his beard tickled her skin.

She blushed. "Th…Thank you, Robert. Sorry I'm late!"

He smiled. "I'd have waited all night for you."

She giggled. "I had to stop off for some money!"

He glanced at his shoes. She noted that they had been shined. For her?

"I feel so bad about having you pay for everything. Just as soon as the job comes through, I'll pay back every penny. I promise!"

He said it with such conviction that she had no choice but to believe him.

The hostess led them to their seats, and Robert helped her with her chair. Such a gentleman!

She didn't speak again until Robert had settled across from her. She watched as he lit his pipe and the pewter-colored smoke rose to the ceiling. He looked so suave. "How was the interview?" she asked.

His face lit up. "Wonderful! I think I'll have a contract by the end of the week."

"Oh, Robert! I'm so happy for you."

He reached across the table and put a hand on hers. "If this book deal works out, I'll be wealthy. We can make quite a life together."

She patted his hand. "And if it doesn't, don't worry. I have seven thousand dollars in the bank. That'll make us a nice start."

He sighed. "But I can't keep taking money from you!"

"We are going to be married soon, right, Robert?"

He shook his head and stared at the half-eaten pasta on his plate. "If only life were so easy, Helen, dear. We have to wait until the contract comes through."

She stiffened. Was she going to lose him because of a silly book contract? "No, Robert!" she blurted. "Contract or not, I want to marry you."

He stared at her for a long moment.

"You're right, sweetheart!" he said slowly. "I can't wait another minute to make you mine! Let's do it tonight! We could go to Las Vegas. It's only a two hour drive, and they'll have us hitched before midnight."

He patted her hand and a smile bloomed slowly on his face. "It'll be wonderful!"

"Yes, my love," she answered. "Then when we get back you'll have your contract and we can move to New York or Hollywood or wherever you want."

Robert wiped his mouth and tossed his napkin on the table. "Dear Helen, let's get going. I promise this will be an unforgettable night."

As she approached the Teller Machine, she nearly stopped walking.

"Hurry, sweetheart!" Robert shouted "The bright lights of Vegas await us."

"Yes, dear."

She inserted her card, and a message appeared on the screen.

WELCOME, MISS WILSON. IT'S NICE TO SEE YOU AGAIN.

She chuckled. "You are so sweet."

WHAT TYPE TRASNSACTION DO YOU WANT?

She pushed the WITHDRAWL FROM CHECKING button.

The computer asked for her PIN code

She entered the numbers.

AMOUNT OF WITHDRAWL?

She typed in the entire amount.

Money started piling up in the tray, then the flow suddenly stopped.

A message appeared on the screen.

ALL OF IT? I CANNOT LET YOU DO THIS, MISS WILSON!

Helen Wilson stepped backward. "I have to. This is my chance for happiness."

DON'T DO THIS!

Robert shouted. "What's the matter, Helen. If that stupid machine doesn't work we can try another one."

Another message.

HE'LL TAKE YOU AWAY. YOU WON'T BE BACK. YOU ARE IN DANGER!

She stared at the note. "Danger?" she whispered. "What kind of danger?"

The screen went black for an instant and a photo appeared. It looked like Robert, younger, without the beard. Below a list began forming. She gasped as she read.

CONVICTED OF ASSAULT WITH INTENT TO HARM – 1982

CONVICTED OF ATTEMPTED MURDER - 1992

VIOLATION OF PAROLE – 1996

WANTED FOR INVESTIGATION OF MURDER - 1999

"Helen! Hurry up!"

"Wait, Robert!"

"What's the problem, anyway?"

"Ah...Just a glitch in the machine."

"Let me see! Maybe I can help?"

HE'S COMING FOR YOU.

She heard the car door open.

"No, Robert! Please! It's okay, now!" She moved back to the machine and grabbed the money. "See, Robert! I've got the cash!"

She heard him walking toward her.

Another message.

TOO LATE. YOU MUST ESCAPE. TURN RIGHT AND RUN TO THE CORNER OF THE BUILDING. HELP IS COMING.

"Escape," she whispered fiercely. "But…!"

"What did you say?" Robert asked. "Let me check it out, Helen!"

His footsteps sounded behind her.

She moaned.

Another message.

HE HAS A GUN! GET AWAY! NOW!

She stumbled sideways, then began to run.

The corner of the building was dark and foreboding.

"Hey! Where are you're going?"

She lost a shoe but kept running. "Stay away from me, Robert!" she shouted.

"Helen! Stop! Come back here!"

She screamed!

"No! Wait, Helen!!" he yelled. His footfalls were loud in her ears. She'd never make the corner.

She screamed and ran faster.

Ahead, a figure in black hurried around the corner.

"Help me!" she shouted. "He has a gun!"

Eyes wide, staring at the two of them, the police officer pulled his weapon, then crouched.

"Police Officer! Drop your weapon!"

Thunder sounded in front of her.

She screamed, then fell to the ground.

"Miss Wilson? Miss Wilson? Are you okay?"

A smell stung her nose. She shook her head. "What? What?"

Her vision cleared. A man in a Fire Department uniform knelt beside her. Official vehicles lined the curb, lights flashing. A crowd had gathered – held back by several policemen.

"Can you hear me okay, Miss Wilson?"

"Yes," she answered slowly. "I think so." Remembering, she sucked in a breath. "Oh my God! What happened?"

Another figure leaned down – a cop. He was smiling.

"You are one lucky woman," he said. "I think that man chasing you wanted to rob you."

"Robert?"

He frowned. "Did you know him?"

"He was my fiancée! Where is he?"

The policeman and medical attendant exchanged glances.

The policeman spoke slowly. "He's dead, ma'am!"

"Dead? Robert?"

"Yes, ma'am! You screamed! You said you were in danger. He was almost on you. I had to act quickly. He must have been a predator."

"That's what the machine said."

"Machine, ma'am?"

"The machine told me about Robert!" she said. "It said he had a record. It said he had a gun!"

The policeman stared at her for a long time. "I heard you screaming. He was chasing you! I had to shoot!"

"Yes! The Teller Machine! It warned me about him!"

"The Automatic Teller?"

"Yes," she said loudly. "Don't you believe me? It warned me. It wouldn't give me all my money."

The policeman held up some cash. "Here's the $300 you were carrying when you fell."

"That's the limit, Miss Wilson," the paramedic added.

"Huh?"

"You can't withdraw more than $300 at a time."

"But...the Automatic Teller said."

The paramedic looked at the cop, who nodded in return. "Well, Miss Wilson. You've had quite a shock. The ambulance will take you to Mercy Hospital. You'll probably remember things differently in the morning. Don't worry, he was running after you all right, and I thought he had a gun, too."

"Thought?"

"Yes, ma'am! It turns out, he was holding his pipe."

"Pipe?" she screamed, "I'm telling you, the Machine told me to run! It said Robert was a danger!"

The officer looked skeptical. "You screamed and ran and called for help because you thought the Automatic Teller warned you?"

She began crying. "Yes! I swear!" Then she screamed. "Robert! Oh, my God!"

The paramedic patted her hand. "I've given you a mild sedative, Miss Wilson. You'll be calmer by the time we get to the hospital."

"But Robert. The Machine."

The attendant popped up the gurney and began wheeling her away. She twisted and strained to see the machine. It looked no different that it did before.

Then she heard the sound.

"Wait!" she screamed. "Stop!"

The Teller clicked furiously. A note appeared on the screen.

"Let me see the message!" she shouted.

The paramedic pushed her to the machine.

WELCOME TO THE BANK OF AMERICA AUTOMATIC TELLER SYSTEM. I LOOK FORWARD TO OUR NEXT TRANSACTION. GOOD NIGHT, AND SLEEP SAFELY, MISS WILSON. TOMORROW, I'LL SUGGEST SOME INVESTMENTS.

Helen Wilson screamed again. "You killed Robert! I hate you! I'll never come back!"

The screen went black.

As the attendant pushed her toward the ambulance, the police office ran up. Colored lights reflected from his face giving him a surreal quality. "Miss Wilson! Miss Wilson! You were right!"

Groggy, she turned her head in his direction.

He stopped beside her. "We just removed Robert's jacket. Sure enough, he had a gun tucked in there. Serial numbers filed off and everything. And his wallet had three fake IDs." He smiled. "He's a bad one, all right. Your intuition saved you."

"Intuition?"

"Sure thing! No other way to account for it."

She settled backward onto the gurney, then smiled at the attendant as he lifted her into the back of the ambulance.

"Do you think he'll forgive me?"

"Who?" the man asked. "That dead creep?"

"No!" She giggled. "The Automatic Teller. I was very rude to it just now, wasn't I?"

TEEN AVENGER

He tapped his cigarette against the grimy ashtray. Steal-colored smoke traced a loping arc toward the stained ceiling. He watched it briefly - and waited. He loved the waiting. It was like fishing. Bait the hook. Toss it out. Wait for the bite. Reel 'em in. He had a good feeling about this one.

His monitor screen displayed a message.

I'm on. Is this Wildchild?

His grimy fingers danced across the keyboard and a smile lit his features.

Yeah! Is this Hotstuff?

Always!

Great! He typed. *I wasn't sure about you.*

No, man! I'm okay with this!

F-ing A Hotstuff! Man, your parents sound like creeps!

The worst!

Mine too! Always putting me down.

So, Wildchild, what did you want to tell me?

You sounded cute and so mature. It's hard to meet anyone cool over the net.

Tell me about it – Too many weirdoes!!!!!

Right! He chuckled as he typed. *I mean, you could be some fat chic looking for computer sex, or a narc, or worse yet a sick old man posing to get his jollies.*

LOL!!! Gross! Not me, man!

Me either!

Conversation paused. It was always this way with empty-headed teenagers. Bursts of stupid conversation, then nothing for minutes. But he knew the drill. The hook was in. Couldn't pull too hard or the nubile little fish would be lost.

He typed slowly. *So what were you doing at the Nirvana site, Hotstuff?*

I love Kirk.

Me too! What a drag – him dead and all!

Yeah*! You think they killed him?*

Sure they did! They were afraid!

No shit! His message was too loud.

He took a long drag on his cigarette. How old was she? Thirteen – fourteen tops. Probably from a broken home. Mother overly permissive. Gangly. No boyfriends. Can't carry on a conversation with an adult. It all added up to - Easy Target!

He typed. *Hey! You don't have a boyfriend do you?*

No way! Why?

You sound like a hottie. I don't want to waste my time.

All the boys up here are dorks!

The girls here are the same!

Oh! Mom's coming! Gotta go!

I'll be on-line later - Hotstuff!

See 'ya!

He smiled. So far, so good! Tonight about midnight she'd be back on line.

Sandy Horrohan shook her head emphatically, and her dark shoulder-length hair swished across her face. "I wish you'd, like, stop this, Kara. It's got to be illegal!"

Kara Charles scoffed. "What? Do you think they'd prosecute a teenage girl?"

"It's like, you know, I don't want to get in trouble, Kara!"

Kara smoothed back her long blonde hair as she spoke. "Come on Sandy! We're doing the world a favor. Let's run an analysis and see what comes out?"

Kara saved the Internet conversation as 'Wildchild-Target-23' then opened the program titled *Lingo-Analysis Prototype*.

"Analyze this!" she said, and punched the 'Enter' button.

"Man," Sandy remarked. "It's, like, amazing, you know, what your dad can do with computers."

Kara nodded. "Yeah! And him being on the University staff really helps."

"You're gonna get him fired, you know."

"No way! Besides, I helped him program this. I know what I'm doing."

The computer buzzed and a screen message appeared.

THE ANALYSIS IS COMPLETED

Kara smiled. "See! Piece of cake, Sandy!"

She punched the 'Enter' button again.

The screen message changed.

THE ANALYSIS IS CORRECT TO A 95% DEGREE OF ACCURACY.

PROBABLE IDENTITY OF PARTIES:
- **WILDCHILD – MALE**
- **HOTSTUFF – FEMALE**

"Spooky!" Sandy whispered. "How does the program, like, figure that out?"

"My dad says males and females have way different speech patterns. His program distinguishes them."

PROBABLE AGES OF PARTIES:
- **WILDCHILD – FOURTY**
- **HOTSTUFF - MIDTEENS**

"Forty!" Sandy shouted. "Like, Gross! He's ancient!"

Kara chuckled. "Naughty, naughty, Mister Wildchild!"

PROBABLE EDUCATION LEVEL OF PARTIES:
- **WILDCHILD – 12TH GRADE**
- **HOTSTUFF – 9TH GRADE**

"Hey!" Kara shouted. "I'm in 10th Grade!"

They both laughed.

Kara leaned back in the seat. "So! Wildchild is a voueuyer."

Sandy frowned. "What's that mean?"

"He likes to see girls like us naked – or worse! Probably sells the photos or posts them on the web for profit."

"That is sooooo gross, Kara!" She looked down at herself. "It's like, you know, I don't even like to see me naked."

They laughed again.

She typed.

You there Wildchild?

Man, I live on-line, Hotstuff!

Tell me more, great guru.

It's midnight and I'm lonely – that's one thing I can sure say.

Oh, God – Me Toooooo!

So, What do you look like?

Why's it important?

So I can imagine 'ya when we're chatting!

Well, I'm beautiful for one thing – a future supermodel. And I'm the greatest brain to ever attend King Junior High. I am also Miss Popularity. How about you?

I'm just nobody! If you're beautiful, I guess there's no hope for us.

Maybe.

So...Send me your picture!

Aw, that's a barf-out, man!

Come on! Please! I gotta see how beautiful you look!

Why?

Because I need a friend – someone cool like you.

That's sad!

Yeah. Girls don't like me – They think I'm too weird 'cause I think too much!
I might like weird guys!
Sure! But you won't even send me a picture.
Okay! I'll do it! I have a digital Dad took at my last birthday.
That's great, Hotstuff! I've never known a supermodel before.
LOL. About that…maybe I lied a little.
I'll bet you didn't!
OK Wildchild! One photo coming up!!!!

"I kind of, like, feel sorry for him, Kara."
"Not me! Whose photo should I send?"
Sandy laughed. "You're terrible! But, like, if you ask me – how about Susan Hoyt?"
"Cheerleader Susan? That'll get him stirred up for sure!"
Sandy giggled. "Send him the one, you know, from the Yearbook - her in the hot pants."

He typed.
Oh, man! You are a knockout! I'm having naughty thoughts right now!
Stop it!
Man! You're not some holy roller are you?
No way!
Maybe we could go together?
So soon?
Why not? It seems right to me!
My mom won't let me go out.
Oh! Mommy says so, huh?
Hey! It's not like that! I'm one independent babe!
But you can't go out with me?
I guess – If I want!

I printed your photo. I'll tape it over my bed tonight!
That's so sweet!
I feel so happy. You are the greatest! Do you have more pictures?
Some!
I'll bet you don't have the kind I mean?
What's that!
Something, you know - hot – from Hotstuff!
Like what?
Like something – maybe a little - naughty!
Like naked? No way!
Come on! We're a couple! One photo!
You'll pass it around school!
Oh, my God! Never! You're my girl now.
I don't think so!
Please! Nobody ever paid this much attention to me before.
Well!
You're dad has a digital camera?
Sure!
Use it real quick! Send it JPEG. You won't regret it, I promise.
I don't know!
Hurry! I need you. You're my Hotstuff!
It might take a while!
I'll be waiting!

Sandy sighed. "I am, like, so grossed out!"

"Me too!" Kara said. "Shall I engage the final phase to this operation?"

"Like, do it! Hose him!"

"One hosing coming up!"

Sandy giggled. "This is so illegal."

Kara slipped a disk into the hard drive. "Attach my program – and 'Send'."

She pressed the button and the computer beeped.

The ashtray overflowed. He had just finished communicating with another one.

"You've got Mail!"

He smiled. "So soon! This is just too easy."

"If the little bitch really looks like that photo," he mumbled, "I'm gonna make a mint. Soooo sexy!" There was a file attached to the E-Mail.

He clicked to open it and the standard warning message appeared.

This is a warning. It is sometimes inadvisable to open mail from unknown sources. Open anyway?

He chuckled. "Inadvisable? Not this mail! Come to papa!"

He clicked the 'Open' button.

The computer chugged. Almost immediately a message appeared on the screen.

This is it!

The computer continued chugging.

Just what you asked for – and what you deserve!

He frowned. Pretty damn sophisticated for a silly little girl.

The computer beeped.

Attention Scumbag! You've been tagged by the Teen Avenger. Your hard drive has been compromised. Do not attempt to shut down the computer or interfere in any way or you will lose all data. The virus program has now copied and forwarded personal information. I know who you are! Do not attempt further contact or your secret will be revealed.

As Kara Charles studied the data, her demeanor changed.

"Did you get it all?" Sandy asked.

"Ahhhh...Enough!"

"So, who is it?"

Kara hesitated. "We don't want to know!"

Sandy grabbed at the papers and laughed. "Yes, I do. Who's the scumbag?"

Kara tried to pull the papers away, but they spilled onto the floor. Sandy pounced on several sheets. "Who is it?" she giggled. "Come on. Tell me!"

"Sandy! Stop!"

Sandy lifted a sheet of paper and turned away from Kara to read it.

Sandy was quiet for several seconds, then dropping the papers on the floor, she turned. "It's not true! You made it up!"

"I'm sorry, Sandy. I didn't know."

Sandy paused. Her eyes welled up. "Oh, daddy, how could you?"

VISIONS

"Can you hear me, Mister Kazmerek?"

Tired eyes evaluated me before the old man nodded.

"I've come from the Archdiocese to speak to you."

A smile touched a corner of his wizened mouth. "I knew dey'd send someone."

"Then you know why I'm here?"

"It's the visions, Father, ain't that right?"

I moved a chair beside his hospital bed, sat on the very edge, and looked around. The open bay wing of the facility was mostly quiet. Most other patients were in the solarium or at activities. "How long have you been here, Mister Kazmerek?"

"Here? Where am I, Father? I woke 'bout two weeks ago, but ain't been talking much – waiting for ya - and they leaves me alone."

"You are in the Crownsville Medical Facility."

"The Nut House! Why'd dey put me here?"

"For your safety, Mister Kazmerek."

"'Cause I was drinkin'?"

"I talked to your neighbors in Locust Point. They say you were drunk for two straight weeks. Raving and incoherent. They were afraid you would kill yourself."

"Well, that's none of 'em's business." He pointed to the table beside me. "Can ya get me a glass a wooder?"

This wasn't going as I expected. I poured a glass, handed it to the old man, then smiled. "Let's start over, Mister Kazmerek." I reached out a hand. "I'm Father Michael McHale. I've been sent by the Archbishop to speak to you about your letter."

Kazmerek took a sip, eyed the glass distastefully, then smiled knowingly. "She said it would get your attention."

"She?"

He watched me closely as he answered. "The Virgin. She said dey'd have ta send someone."

I straightened in the chair. "Are you referring to the Blessed Mother?"

"Yes, Father. It's her what speaks ta' me."

I had watched him. He showed none of the typical signs of lying. His face didn't redden. His jaw muscles didn't clench. His eyes didn't twitch. I had been a police detective for ten years before joining the Jesuits. I had seen enough liars in that time to recognize the signs. He believed what he said.

"Are you of Portuguese descent, Mister Kazmerek?"

His laughter echoed throughout the ward and caused several other patients to stop their activities and stare at us. Kazmerek hacked and coughed until I was afraid he couldn't breathe. I signaled for a nurse.

A heavy black lady arrived at the bedside within seconds. She sat the old man up and patted his back expertly.

"Now Mister K. It's nice to see you active, but it won't look so good if you go choking on us, now will it? Want some wooder?"

Kazmerek shook his head as he calmed. The nurse cranked up the bed so he was nearly sitting, then settled into a chair on the opposite side from me as she took his pulse.

"Did you say Portugee?" He addressed me.

"Yes. Is your ancestry Portuguese?"

"It's the letter, ain't it?"

"The letter was written in an archaic form of Portuguese," I replied. " How did you do that?"

"I'm a Pollock, Father, like most of 'em in the 'Point. She tol' me what ta write. Letter by letter. I wrote like she said."

I took out my note pad – the same one I had used on the Baltimore City Police force. "Okay, Mister Kazmerek. Let's start from the beginning."

I watched Father McHale as he waited for me to begin. It was jus' like the Virgin said. They'd come when I wrote. I liked the priest. He weren't so old so's to be hard-headed, but he weren't so young so's to be foolish. The Lady would be pleased.

"I guess I've always had a like'en for the bottle ever since Vietnam," I began. "Mostly beer. But, once in a while I get a cravin' for a stiff one."

"I retired from the waterfront in 1999. Worked right up to my 65th year. There ain't much ta do in Locust Point if ya ain't working – 'cept drinking. There's enough bars there for sure – and churches."

I turned to the nurse. "What's your name, hon?"

She smiled. "Clarisse."

"Ya' ever been ta Locust Point, Miss Clarisse?"

She laughed. "No dear. I stay close to Cherry Hill and my grandkids."

"You should go down there. It's a special place. Most folks raised there never leaves it."

I turned toward Father McHale. "'Bout 6 months ago, I got half a load on down at *Hull Street Blues* and started wanderin' the neighborhood. For some reason I sat down on the steps at Our Lady of Good Counsel Church – don't know why."

Father McHale narrowed his gaze and I began hastily. "I ain't a bad Catholic, Father. I go 'ta Mass most holidays. Take Communion Easter and Christmas. Anyways, I got thinkin' 'bout Church and wondered if I could go inside and pray. God knows I need it. I knew they locked the door these days, but I tol' God that if the door wuz open, I'd pray up a storm."

I touched the sleeve of Father's cassock. "It wuz open!"

"So I went in, marched right up the altar, and knelt – the old fashioned way. That's when it happened."

Father watched me, then spoke. "What happened, Mister Kazmerek?"

"Ya' ever been in Good Counsel Church, Father?"

He shook his head.

"It's a nice old place. Kinda comfortable. Well they got this statue of the virgin – life size - in a shrine on one side the altar 'an a statue 'a Saint Joseph on da' other. Anyways, once I started prayin', the statue of Mary spoke 'ta me."

"How did it speak?" Father asked.

"The sweetest voice. Female a'course."

"What did she say?"

I stared at my hands and hesitated. "Now 'ya see. That's the hard part. She wuz talkin' and I wuz listenin', and it made sense the whole time, but when I got home, I couldn't 'member it all. I tried, but it weren't clear no more."

I watched Father's face. He didn't believe. That wuz okay. She said they'd be hard ta convince.

"Then what?" he asked.

"I went back the next evening, but the door wuz locked, so I went to Sherry's and had a few stiff ones. On the way home, I stopped by the Church again." I looked at them again. "Swear 'ta God! The doors wuz open!"

Father spoke. "You heard her again?"

"Same as before. 'Cept this time I was drunker and I remembered it all the way home. Even had time 'ta write it down."

I reached under my pillow and pulled out a sheet of paper. My scribbling filled both sides. I handed it to Father. "I always keep the notes with me – 'jus in case. They wuz in my pocket when the ambalance brought me here." I felt a sense of pride sweep over me. "I am chosen, Father, ain't I? I'm a prophet!"

I examined Kazmerek's paper. The drunken scrawl swept at an angle across the page. Some of it was legible – barely. As near as I could make out, the writing announced a time of great trouble, the fall of a powerful leader, and a hint of the anti-Christ. We'd need a handwriting analysis to get much more from this scribble.

I returned the notes. "Very interesting, Mister Kazmerek. Is there more?"

He nodded slyly. "Oh, yeah! Plenty!"

"What do you know of the Book of Revelations?"

"That's the Bible, huh?"

I waited.

"Well, bein' Catholic," he answered. "I ain't found much time for the Bible, 'cept for what they read at Mass."

"Please, continue," I said.

Kazmerek took a sip of water, then winced. "I went back the next ten nights, each time drunker. She talked to me, Father. The drunker I wuz, the more I understood. I stayed drunk all day 'jus so's I could keep 'ta the feelings. It was harder each time, but I kept it up. I was almost at the final answer when they took me away."

"You were vomiting blood in your kitchen sink, Mister K," Clarisse interrupted. "You were in bad shape– still are."

He pulled more sheets of paper from under his pillow and handed them to me.

I read them quickly. They were all the same type predictions. Earthquakes, Flood, Fires, Starvations, Wars. Easy to predict in general terms. I returned them to the old man. "Nothing more specific, Mister Kazmerek?"

He laughed again. "She said you'd need better proof, all right." He turned toward Clarisse. "What's today, hon?"

"July 6th," Clarisse answered.

He removed another sheet of paper. "On the 8th there will be a major airplane crash. An earthquake will strike Taiwan. And the Orioles will lose to Boston."

I laughed. "The Orioles always lose to Boston, Mister Kazmerek. And the rest of the predictions seem somewhat vague - anyone could make them."

Kazmerek smiled. "Come back on the 8th, Father, and we can talk again. But I need ya' ta' get me out a here. Ah'm the Prophet. I wuz close to figurin' it all out when they hauled me in. The Virgin needs me." He paused. "An I need ta git drinkin'."

Eyes watering, he smiled at me. "One more thing about the 8th, Father?" He paused. "You mom is real sick, ain't she?"

"Yes," I answered suddenly angry that he had brought my family into his confused picture. "How did you know?"

"The Virgin says she'll pass on to Jesus on the 8th in the mornin'. You should get back ta Pikesville 'ta be with her tomorra'."

Clarisse gasped.

I stared at Kazmerek. It was impossible for me to hide my anger. "The Virgin Mary told you this?" I said loudly.

"See you on the 8th, Father. I'll have an important message for the Pope. Come in the afternoon, once ya made the arrangements. Sorry about your mom."

I left the room in a rush - anger and fear at war within me. I used language in my head I had not used since I left the Police Force.

Father McHale approached my bed. "Thank you, Mister Kazmerek."

I watched the Priest to see if he were tellin' the truth. It seemed so.

"She took a turn for the worst yesterday," he continued, "and died peacefully this morning. I was with her all day, thank God."

"God bless you, Father," Clarisse whispered.

Father McHale nodded to her.

I continued. "And I guess you heard about that horrible crash in South America, and that China quake too?"

Father McHale laughed. "And the Orioles lost 8 to zip."

I extended the envelope to Father. In it was the last message from the Virgin. "She said this would be the final proof, but it has to get to the Pope. Only he can see it. She needs an answer in three days. I gotta be out a here by then, Father."

"Why?"

"So I can git good and drunk. I can't miss the final message."

Clarisse spoke up. "Prophet you may be, Mister Kazmerek, but you can't drink no more. You know what the Doctor said. Your systems are failing. It'll kill you, as sure as I'm sitting here."

I stared at the envelope, suddenly afraid.

Kazmerek must have sensed my apprehension. He extended the envelope farther, until it touched my hand. "It'll be okay," he said. "The Virgin tol' me."

I took a deep breath, took the envelope, and quickly put it inside my valise. I could feel the ominous presence of the envelope as I drove to the Archdiocese offices.

I hadn't expected a reaction so quickly. Archbishop Cornell and Bishop Braham called me late the following morning. They had commissioned a Seminarian to hand-deliver the envelope, and I had seen him off at Dulles Airport early yesterday evening on an Al-Italia flight direct to Rome.

I drove carefully to the meeting. My excitement had been building. I had also spent all my free time over the last several days reading the old manuscripts concerning the Final Days and particularly The Book of Revelations.

The Bishops appeared solemn. Both wore their dark robes with red piping. This was official – and very unusual. "Please be seated, Michael," Bishop Braham said.

I took a seat in one of the plush chairs that graced the Archbishop's Office. Both priests stared at me. Finally the Archbishop made a deliberate sign of the cross. "In the name of the Father, the Son, and the Holy Spirit." I recited in time with them.

"In accordance with Cannon Law, I must ask for your vow of silence on what I am about to reveal, Father McHale. Treat this as you would a confession."

"Our confession," Bishop Braham added.

Archbishop Cornell opened an envelope sitting in the center of his desk, wax seal broken - the papal seal. He removed a letter, and placed it on the desk in front of him.

"We passed on the information about Mister Kazmerek, Father. The visions, the predictions, the fact of your mother's death. Rome is naturally skeptical – there are many hoaxes and hoaxers in this word – and outside of it; but the Holy Father is always alert to the voice of God. His staff was anxious to see what you had."

He pointed to the letter. "The Holy See has examined the letter and concluded that with reasonable certainty, that Mister Kazmerek has access to information only the highest officials in Rome could know."

He folded his hands in front of him on the desk.

I hadn't realized I had been holding my breath. "Then," I sputtered, "this is a bona-fide Vision?"

The Bishop shook his head. "Not so fast, Michael. It'll take a few hundred years before the Church makes any official declaration." He raised his eyebrows. "But, the Papal staff is intrigued. A Commission has been formed. Investigators are on their way."

"God bless us! That's incredible!"

The Archbishop interrupted. "There's more."

My spirits sank. Something wasn't right.

"It appears," The Archbishop continued, "that the message wasn't complete. The final revelation is not finished. Rome needs more information."

"Kazmerek gave me all he had," I answered.

"It wasn't everything the vision wanted to say."

I stared from priest to priest. "What can I do?"

"Take Kazmerek back to Good Council," the Bishop said.

This was not the direction I had been expecting. "But," I sputtered, "his body is failing. He may die."

The Archbishop shook his head. "He'll have to do it without the alcohol."

"He truly believes he needs alcohol to get the message!"

"All life is risk, Father McHale. There are no easy answers. Jesus took the greatest risk and paid with his life."

"Maybe I could take Kazmerek's place?"

Braham laughed. "Oh, I'd love to see you rip-roaring drunk, Michael, but it wouldn't do any good."

"Why not?"

"Kazmerek is chosen, Father. It's his cross to bear."

"Then what do I do?"

Bishop Braham spoke quietly. "Pray hard, Father. We will do the same. Tomorrow, arrange with the Hospital to release Kazmerek to you for the day. Take him to Locust Point. God has entrusted you with this situation. He will show you the way."

When I entered the Ward, I could feel something was wrong. I rushed to Kazmerek's bed and pulled back the privacy curtain. The bed was empty! I felt the blood drain from my head. I nearly fell down. "Clarisse!" I shouted. "Where is he?"

I searched the hospital and the grounds. I found Clarisse sitting in an outdoor arbor watching the clouds. She didn't look at me, but she knew I was there.

"What happened, Clarisse?"

"Mister Kazmerek knew you were coming."

"How did he know that?"

"He said She told him."

I felt a shudder. I suddenly knew more than I wanted. "Where is he?"

"He begged me to let him go. I wouldn't. Finally he said he would give me information about my grandbabies. He said one of them was bound for prison unless I intervened. He knew which one and what to do. I knew it too."

"Where is he, Clarisse?

"I bought him some booze, then took him to Locust Point – to the church." Tears welled up in her eyes. "I am so sorry, Father."

I put a hand on her head. "I know you are, Clarisse. God forgives you."

The drive to Baltimore took me 30 minutes. Traffic was heavy, and I didn't have a cell phone to contact the Archdiocese. When I arrived, the doors of Good Counsel Church stood open revealing a dark and foreboding interior.

The church was built on the old style with an altar in the center front and pews aligned along a central aisle. At first I thought the church was empty, but it was hard to see after the bright exterior. As I moved forward, my hard-soled shoes made slapping noises on the terrazzo floor that echoed harshly. Then I saw – legs - Kazmerek lying near the shrine to the Blessed Virgin. Candles blazed in the red glass holders in front of Mary's statue. An empty bottle of Whiskey lay on the floor beside him. I ran to him, all the while watching the statue, half expecting it to come alive.

I lifted his head into my arms. "Mister Kazmerek! Can you hear me?"

His body convulsed, then he opened his eyes. "Father?"

"Yes! It's me."

"I did it, Father." He glanced to his left, and I noticed a leaf of paper on the floor half-hidden by his body.

"She gave it ta' me. I am the Prophet."

I looked at the statue. "God bless you, Mister Kazmerek."

He smiled, then closed his eyes for a final time. I felt his arm, but only confirmed that his pulse had stopped.

I reached into my pocket and removed the tiny vial containing the Holy Chrism. Praying the words I so often dreaded, I anointed the old man – his Last Rites.

I picked up the papers from the floor, and put everything into my valise. Then I went to my car, opened the trunk, I brought out the items I had packed earlier. Before I returned to the church, I stopped a passer-by with a cell phone clinging to his ear. "Call an ambulance. Someone has had a heart attach inside the church."

I had to work fast. I slipped on my Roman collar, set the bell, book, holy water, and candles in their place, then faced the statue. "You picked an old man for your revelations and you gave him secret information. But there are two sides to the spiritual world, and our side would never sacrifice a single human life for its own purposes. I know who you are."

I raised my arms and sprinkled the holy water on and around the statue, all the while shouting. "I cast thee out!" "I cast thee out!" "I cast thee out!"

Despite my lack of formal training, I had read up for this eventuality. I picked up the book and recited the Latin Rite of Exorcism, slowly, methodically. By the time the ambulance arrived I was sweating and near exhaustion. But I knew I had been successful.

The paramedics pronounced Mister Kazmerek dead at the scene. I touched him on the chest before they put him on the gurney. "Go with God, Mister Kazmerek. You fought the good fight."

Archbishop Cornell seemed surprised to see me. He and Bishop Braham had been in prayer when I arrived. I was ready. I had been up all night praying, preparing, and I had had a revelation of my own. Despite the lack of sleep, I felt heady.

"Kazmerek is dead." I announced.

The Bishop winced. "I am so sorry!"

Cornell spoke excitedly. "You took him to the church?"

"No Your Eminence. He escaped the Institution."

"Then how…?"

"He bribed a nurse with information. She helped him." I paused for a few moments. "I exorcized the statue!"

Bishop Cornell watched me closely. "So, you decided that this was the work of the Dark One?"

I nodded. "It had to be."

"Did Kazmerek get the information he spoke of?"

"The Great Temptations are prophesized, Archbishop."

"You didn't answer my question, Father."

My answer came in a rush of words – too fast. "Mister Kazmerek had consumed an entire bottle of whiskey in less than an hour and died before he could write anything."

The Archbishop stared at me. He knew I was lying. I didn't care.

"Then, did he speak?" Bishop Braham asked. "This is vital. Did he say anything we can pass on?"

"Only to mumble that he had found the answer." I watched them. "Besides," I added, "it was all lies intended to deceive us and to influence the Holy See."

"Such a shame," Bishop Braham said. "To have died for nothing."

"Not for nothing, Your Eminence," I answered. "We know now that the battle has been joined."

Cornell stared at me. "Even so, Father. To know the enemy's lies might tell us much about his intentions. It would have been powerful information for the Holy Father."

He wanted me to tell him everything. But no! "It's too late now," I snapped.

He watched me for what seemed like a minute before answering. "I hope not, Father. For all our sakes."

I shoved my hands deep into my pockets and stared at him, unspeaking, waiting.

He sighed. "The Holy Father's message mentioned another thing. One we didn't speak of yesterday."

Still I waited. I found myself smiling. I knew what power lay waiting in my pocket – if only I was brave enough to master it.

The Archbishop's words were hard. "There have been other 'Revelations' recently." He looked at his hands, folded neatly across the front of his cassock. "Priests have been corrupted by the knowledge, Father. Just like the Garden." He looked up at me. "There is some knowledge men are not meant to possess."

I clenched my hidden hands and the sound of crumpling paper filled the still air. My answer was arrogant – and strangely out of character. "Even you, Archbishop?"

Bishop Braham's eyes hardened. His voice trembled. "You are so transparent, Father. Look what's happened to you. The Church must have that information!"

"You'll never have it!" I turned and strode from the room.

My breath was labored as I approached the altar, staring at the empty chalice. My legs didn't seem to want to move. I fought back panic. I had returned to Good Counsel Church after dark – and the door was open.

I stopped at the edge of the altar and put both hands, palms down, on the marble top. My vision blurred and I waited for it to clear.

Slowly, I removed the papers from my pocket and spread them out on the altar, careful not to look at the words. Those haunting words. Those words of power that would surely corrupt me if I so much as read even one.

Fighting incredible rages, I picked up the first sheet, eyes closed. The sounds of ripping echoed throughout the Church. One by one I shred the pages and put the pieces into the chalice. Then I lit the match.

I knelt before the upholstered chair and folded my hands. "Bless me, Father, for I have sinned…"

"Have you, Michael?"

"You know I have, Your Eminence."

"God forgives all sins, my son."

"I disobeyed a request of the Pope, Your Eminence."

He chuckled. "Over the years many people have done likewise."

"The message killed one man, Your Holiness. It almost made me disavow my immortal soul. It had begun to possess me. I had to destroy it."

He nodded. "God knows, I hope you did the right thing."

"Only God knows," I answered.

SHARPER THAN THE SERPENT'S TOOTH

"I'm telling you, Detective Brubeck, it's just not possible!"

I watched Doctor Joshua Moses's ruddy face, waiting for the telltale signs that this was a joke. He had that reputation. But his look remained troubled, and I didn't like that. I wanted things all tied up in neat packages.

I held up the document I had brought down from the Amarillo Sheriff's Office. "You say impossible? Now that's a pretty unusual word, coming from an educated man like yourself - especially when your own Autopsy says different."

Doc Moses shook his head. His silver hair, plastered in place by some miracle of modern coiffure, didn't move. I wondered if he were wearing a hairpiece. When he spoke again, his voice was thick with West Texas angst. "You know, son," he drawled. "I been in this business more than 30 years. Thought I'd seen everything – 'til this."

"Your report," I interrupted, "Says that Mister Jeremiah Clanton died from snake venom. Is that true?"

"Yes, sir. It is! No question 'bout it!"

"What kind of snake, Doc?"

He raised his voice. "Like my Report says – rattlers!"

"He was bit? You're sure?"

Moses weathered, sunburned face became noticeably more red. "It's all there in writing, Detective. Yes! He was bit!"

"How many bites did you count?"

"I stopped counting when I got to a hundred."

I nodded. "Now that there's the part that got my attention. See I was born in Amarillo just like you. I know the desert. I've had encounters with rattlers. Even got bit once. But, a hundred times…? A rattler can't eat a human. Scare him? Sure! So what's the point to a hundred bites?"

"More than that!"

"What?"

"I stopped counting at a hundred. There were many more bites than that!"

I looked at the Report. "Doc, I'm supposed to advise the Sheriff. But nothing in this Report makes sense to me."

Moses shrugged. "It makes no sense to me either. But the Report is accurate."

"How many snakes did we gather up at the scene?"

He thought for a second. "I think thirty. All of 'em dead."

"Thirty dead snakes?"

"Yep!"

I pondered. "I thought a rattler usually only bit once?"

"Far as I know that's true."

"Thirty snakes – more than a hundred bites. So how am I going to account for this slight mathematical discrepancy, Doc?"

Moses shrugged. "Can't help you there, but I have a theory."

I watched his face closely. "What is it, Doc?"

He chuckled. "You'll never get a herpetologist to testify to this, but I think the snakes bit Mister Clanton multiple times."

"Multiple times?"

"Yep," he answered. "In fact, I think the rattlers bit him until they ran out of venom." He paused. "Then they kept biting til they died of exhaustion!"

Sighing, I picked up my white 10-gallon and stuck it on my head tightly. "Thanks for your time."

I turned to depart.

"You going out that way?" he asked.

I stopped, then twisted back to watch him over my shoulder. "What's that?"

"You going out to Titusville to investigate 'The Handlers'?"

"Well, yeah! I gotta get some answers, Doc!"

His face became serious. "Be careful!"

"You think the Resurrectionists are gonna set snakes on me?"

"They are a fervent people. Can't never know what fervent people will do."

I studied the bullet-riddled sign as I entered the City Limits, and headed slowly down Main Street. Titusville, Texas. Population 500. Even by West Texas standards, this was the boonies. Lines of powdery dust slithered across the road in front of me. Tumbleweed piled against the fencing. I passed the local branch of West Texas Savings and Loan, the Rural Post Office, a run-down hotel, and a gas station with a 7/11. The homes that clustered around Main Street were a combination of drab cinder-block boxes and drabber-still house trailers. There weren't many people on the streets, but those that were stopped and watched as I drove past.

The only building with any semblance of civility was the Church of the Resurrectionists. It was bigger than all the other buildings in town, clean, and newly painted. A billboard in front announced:

TITUSVILLE CHURCH OF THE RESURRECTIONISTS
PASTOR: DARYL CLANTON

"Beware God's power, and Fear Not the Serpent, and you shall know the Glorious Resurrection!"

I parked in the gravel lot adjacent to the pastor's home. When I opened the door, a blast of hot, dry air rushed inside and deposited one more layer of dust on the seats and dashboard.

The pastor lived in a mansion compared to the other homes - a two-story wood-framed building with a raked roof. The curtains were drawn tightly and all the windows were closed. I stopped. Something seemed wrong! Oh, yes! Missing was the persistent rumble of air conditioning I had come to expect in Texas summers. I wondered if perhaps the pastor were away on a trip.

Stairs creaked as I approached the door. I pressed the doorbell button firmly.

I could hear the bell sounding inside, but no response. I pressed again, but there was not a single noise of occupancy.

I was about to leave when the door swung open suddenly. Startled, I spun around.

A child, stick-thin, maybe thirteen years old, looked up at me. He was small – no more than five feet tall – and had shaggy dark hair that fell to his shoulders. His eyes were blue and menacing and glinted with something akin to madness.

He held the door as a barrier behind him as he looked me over - amazingly calm for a child his age.

"Can I help, you, officer?" he asked in an unfriendly voice an octave too high.

I tried to look past him into the house, but he purposefully pulled the door closed. This was a cool character. Cool and – Arrogant! The boy not only wasn't afraid that the Law had come to visit, but he was irritated at the interruption.

"Yes, son," I answered using my 'official' voice. "I'm here on an investigation. I'm looking for the Pastor, Daryl Clanton."

Without hesitation, he answered. "I am Daryl!"

I stared at the small boy for a long moment, then spoke slowly. "I'm sorry. You must have misunderstood. I want to speak to your dad - the Pastor here."

"My father is dead," he replied calmly. "I am the new Pastor."

"Your father is Jeremiah Clanton?"

"My father **was** Jeremiah Clanton! Where he is now, he's got a different name."

"And where is that?" I asked. "Where is he?"

The boy cackled shrilly. "My father is burning in the deepest pits of hell! By now, Satan has renamed him as one of his minions."

I felt very uneasy! Without drawing attention to myself, I pretended to adjust my belt, all the while checking to see if the trigger guard on my revolver holster was engaged. It was. I flipped the leather end off the trigger. Better to be safe…

"Well, then," I began, making my voice a little friendlier, "my name is Detective Rufus Brubeck from over in Amarillo. I'm investigating the death of your father. If you're the new Pastor, then it's you I need to talk to. May I come in?"

He hesitated, biting on his lower lip while he considered my request.

"Look…Pastor," I began more firmly. "I'm here as part of an official investigation. I need your cooperation. Where's your mother?"

Again he laughed. "I always suspected that Erleen corrupted my father." He lowered his voice. "She was from Stoney Creek – an outsider, you see. She had too many ideas. My dad called them dangerous. She couldn't handle God's testing."

"What happened to your mother, son…Pastor?"

He smiled. "God found her out. She's dead!"

"Dead? When?"

He smirked. "Three years back – Snake bite!"

I didn't like the direction this conversation was taking, so I changed course. "So, you live by yourself, huh? Well, I need to ask you some questions. Let's go in the house out of this heat."

He smiled as he held open the door for me. "You won't find it much cooler inside, Officer Brubeck. They don't like it cool."

"They?" I asked as I stepped inside, into a wall of incredible cloying heat and a mustiness that prickled my senses – and stopped immediately.

The house was full of snakes! Rattlers! Some moved slowly across the floor, others nestled into slithery bundles, and still others watched me from the furniture, eyes alert, and tongues extended.

Daryl stepped boldly, narrowly missing the tail of an enormous serpent that had crept up to my feet. The snake tasted my snakeskin boots with his tongue. I wondered if that was going to upset the reptile. I put a hand on the butt of my pistol.

"This way," Daryl ordered. "We can talk in the dining room. It's the only place they aren't allowed."

Careful to avoid the creatures, I followed the boy through an open archway into an adjoining room. There was no door, yet not a single snake was in this room.

Daryl offered me a chair. I checked it carefully before I sat. "How many snakes do you have here, Pastor?"

He shrugged. "I never counted."

Remembering some of my early Bible classes, I remarked off-hand. "Haven't numbered the beasts, huh?"

He slapped a hand down onto the tabletop, startling me. "Do not mock my religion. Satan is always vigilant, and he comes in many guises. Knowing the number is not enough!" He eyed me warily. "You might be an agent of the Dark Lord!"

When he said that I noticed frenzied motion out of the corner of my eye. I shifted to observe the doorway. Snakes, hundreds of them, waited ominously just outside the room. They seemed agitated. My heart started racing. The snakes plainly wanted to come inside the room. Something was holding them back! But what? This was way beyond my training. I unholstered my weapon.

Pastor Daryl stared at the revolver for a second, then smiled. "You came in here among the serpents, and all you have is a pistol against God's army?"

I stared at Daryl Clanton. "Son," I said evenly. "You're right! One little pistol against all those snakes would be crazy." I put the gun onto the table. "But against a child who's threatening a Police Officer, I think one bullet will do just fine."

He laughed, and the tone brought shivers to my back. This was not a kid to trifle with. "I'm not afraid to die, Officer. I have passed God's test. I am a Resurrectionist! He will welcome me into his arms."

"If those snakes come any closer, son," I said, patting the revolver. "We're gonna test your little theory." I paused. "Now let's stop the nonsense and talk."

"Fair enough," Daryl said. He took a deep breath and began talking.

Elder Jeremiah Clanton had been the ultimate Pastor, at least as far as the Resurrectionist religion goes. Every Sunday he had preached loudly of brimstone and repentance. He never made the congregation tithe more than 10%. And he could handle the snakes better than anyone in West Texas. According to Daryl, Pastor Jeremiah would dance wildly through the church, praising Jesus so loud the roof would vibrate, and burning the fear of Satin into every heart - all the while balancing rattle snakes in his hands, pockets, shirt, and mouth. Never once was the Pastor bitten in twenty years of snake handling.

"He was God's master of the Serpent," Daryl said, and I detected a note of awe in his voice. "And the Lord protected him."

"Apparently not well enough," I interrupted.

Daryl glared. "Like you," he said, "Pastor Jeremiah - my father - was a prideful man." He stared harder. "Pride goeth before a fall, Officer. My father let the power God gave him turn corrupt, and he was punished for his sins."

"What sins are those?" I asked.

Daryl averted his glance to the tabletop. "Jeremiah's pride turned to lust!"

"Lust!" I said loudly as I removed a pad of paper from my shirt pocket. "Now we're getting somewhere. Tell me more."

"I had a friend about my age," he said, and for the first time a semblance of humility crept into his words. "Her name was Lucinda."

"He let a little senorita charm him, huh?" I asked.

"No! It wasn't like that!" His angry words made me flinch. I heard noises in the doorway, and reached for the pistol.

"Stop!" he shouted in a voice deeper and far more commanding than a child his age could ever rightfully have.

I obeyed. So did the snakes.

Suddenly Daryl was a child. I could see tears forming in his eyes. "She was my friend. I liked her. The Pastor wanted to train her in the 'art' - to be an acolyte." He took a deep, shaky breath before continuing.

"He trained her in lust!" he said, his voice rising in timbre. "She was carrying his child when she died."

"Wait a minute," I said, as I scribbled a note. "Another death? Was this reported?"

"No!" Daryl stared at me. "She was illegal. Her parents were up North somewhere. Since she had been touched by the evil, we buried her in the fields."

"Where?"

He sighed. "Doesn't matter. The snakes scattered her bones. She'll never be found."

I believed him. "Why was she killed, Daryl? Getting pregnant is not a crime in Texas."

"Maybe not in Texas, Officer, but in God's eyes she was the worst kind of sinner. He tested her, and she failed."

"God tested her? Like He did your father – the Pastor?"

Daryl nodded.

"Tell me about it, Daryl."

The Church was packed. It was a Sunday night, unbearably hot. Oppressive wind spit sand against the windows and the air was thick with dust. Every member of the congregation – all the men, women, and even the small children had come.

Six hundred sixty-six burning candles formed a flickering circle of light on the floor in the center of the church.

Pastor Jeremiah stepped to the center of the candle circle and drew the bulging Lucinda after him. His dark brown eyes seemed alive with candle flame. Lucinda's eyes revealed the terror she must have felt. Instinctively she folded her hands over her belly.

"God has given me the gift of the serpents!" Jeremiah shouted toward the ceiling. "You all know that!" Smiling he turned a slow circle and looked at every man in the congregation. "I am the chosen!"

He took one of Lucinda's hands and raised it aloft. "God has given me another gift!" He yelled. "And with this gift the power to finally crush the Evil One!" He looked down at the girl. "This sweet innocent thing bears my child. The child that will lead you through the Apocalypse to Paradise."

Many of the congregation murmured. A woman in the front row shouted. "Sinner!" Others took up the cry.

Pastor Jeremiah dropped Lucinda's hand and held up his own. "NO!" He shouted, "Not a sin!"

"Unclean!" "Harlot!" "Whore Monger!" The cries became fiercer.

"I will show you what God thinks!" Jeremiah shouted angrily. "We will endure God's testing!"

Cries of assent raged throughout the church.

"Bring forth the serpents!" Jeremiah shouted, raising both hands overhead.

As if on cue, the men and boys of the congregation reached into burlap bags, or plastic lunch cartons, or glass terrariums - and brought forth handfuls of snakes. Some were tiny: some enormously long. All vibrated with menace. The sound was frightening - and hypnotizing.

As the men came forward, they danced to a song begun by the women. "Now's the time!" they chanted. "To test the children of God! Now's the time," they sang louder "To vanquish the Beast!"

The men and boys swayed and staggered. Before they had taken a few steps, they were entranced. Several spun in circles as they advanced. Many swayed loosely on rubbery joints. A few cavorted and leapt about.

When the first man came to the candle circle, he held out his snakes. "God Almighty, test these people and reveal their souls to us." With that, he flung the serpents into the circle. Toward the Pastor and the now-screaming Lucinda.

The second man did the same. And the third. The fourth. On and on it went until the floor inside the circle writhed with snakes.

Unwilling to cross the line of candles, the snakes slithered about on top of each other, but none of them approached Jeremiah.

Lucinda huddled against the Pastor, her screams muffled by his shirt.

"Sinners!" The shout caused the Pastor to look up.

Daryl stood just outside the circle. He face was a mask of rage and hate. "Sinners!" He shouted again, and the Pastor faltered.

"God punishes!" Daryl screamed. "You have the mark of the Beast upon you!"

The Pastor looked at the snakes for the first time.

The floor was covered - four serpents thick. Every snake faced the couple. And now they started slithering, slowly at first, then faster, toward him.

"God will protect me!" Jeremiah screamed, but his voice had lost its authority.

"You are a sinner!" Daryl screamed. "God will cast you out this night!"

The snakes reached them. Jeremiah looked at his son, fear peeling his eyelids backward so that the whites shone brightly in the candlelight.

Lucinda screamed. A snake had attached itself to her leg just above the ankle. Another joined the first. Soon her legs were covered in writhing forms. Crying out, she fell to her knees.

Eyes wide with fear, she looked at Pastor Jeremiah, then fell to the floor - to be covered in a roiling mass of snakes.

Jeremiah watched her sink, then he too cried out. A snake slithered from under the collar of his shirt. It sank fangs into his neck. He screamed again. More snakes clung to his clothes, slunk into his pants and shirt. He fell.

Daryl turned to the congregation. "God has chosen to punish the wicked!" he screamed. "The Beast is vanquished!"

"Pastor Daryl! Pastor Daryl! Pastor Daryl!"

"We took Pastor Jeremiah's body," Daryl said, "and dumped it in the middle of the Amarillo Highway, covered with dead snakes - as an example to all sinners."

I pondered. "What you people did was murder," I said.

"What we did was retribution! God made the choice! The snakes were his instruments!"

"But your father is dead!" I said incredulously.

"My father was a sinner! The congregation is purged."

I watched his face before speaking, "Sharper than the serpent's tooth, Daryl!"

He frowned. "What?"

"Something I remember from High School Shakespeare. 'Sharper than the serpent's tooth are the words of an ungrateful child.'"

He nodded and smiled.

"I'm going to have to report this," I said.

"Go ahead! What will the authorities do? Nothing!"

"Maybe. Maybe not!" I picked up the revolver and stood.

Snakes blocked my exit.

"They'll let you go," Daryl said quietly. "You do not carry the Mark."

I started forward. The wall of snakes parted before me and I trod carefully down the middle of the floor.

"If they send someone else," Daryl said as I reached the door, "make sure they don't tryst with Satan. In my church the serpents are God's army. They know their own kind, Officer. The serpents always know!"

BY THE BUCKET

"There's this old guy, see?" The caller hesitated. "And every night I seen 'em hauling a bucket down the end a Hull Street."

"A bucket?"

"Yeah. Big one – like the painters use."

"And what does he do?"

"Dumps it in the wooder."

"But you can't see what it is?"

"Nah! I just watch, is all."

"Is that everything?"

He almost yelled at me. "Yeah! That's all! Ain't it enough?"

"Well, thank you for your tip."

"I mean," he continued. "Christ knows what he's dumping, huh?"

"Yes, sir. Thank you."

"It might poison stuff, right?"

"Yes, sir. Good bye." I hung up.

Normally the Ecology Department would have assigned a junior scientist, but ever since the mayor appointed that Glowacki woman to run things, I'd been relegated to the shit jobs. Ten years of enforcement, and I was still doing field work no one else wanted to touch. I was plenty ticked at my predicament.

I looked at my watch as I pulled into the parking area - 9 PM. The summer sun had just set. A spectacular July evening – warm, but not too muggy. Across the way, neon lights from the National Aquarium danced rhythms of color on the glassy water, happy crowds streamed across the wide plazas of the Inner Harbor, and muffled cheers drifted in the air from Camden

Yards. There was a time when I would have enjoyed this, but the Locust Point side of the Harbor was still undeveloped, and I would have to endure the odor of fuel oil, creosote, - and decay.

Two young lovers paused near the far edge of the pier. They merged briefly - an embrace of groping shadows. I chuckled. No pollution there. Then I settled against the seat of the pick-up truck – and waited.

I had fallen asleep – a deep rest that I seldom get any more. A sound had disturbed me. The noise came again – a low grunt followed by a shuffling. I checked my watch – nearly midnight. Damn! So late! And I had work in the morning.

Sitting up, I noted the shadow that moved slowly under the foliage of an overhanging elm. It was a small shape, toting something heavy. Must be the culprit.

I paused an extra few seconds. Watching. Listening.

Soundlessly, I clipped my badge to my shirt pocket, put my revolver in the shoulder holster, then slipped from the truck.

At the foot of the pier, I stopped and watched. A man, maybe in his late sixties, had stopped near the end of the pier, where he was illuminated by the bluish light cast from the sodium fixture. No was else was nearby. The man was small – slightly more than five feet tall, and very frail in appearance. He held tightly to the handle of a white bucket. Water sloshed to the pier deck with every labored step. Whatever he carried must have been heavy.

He put the bucket down, stretched his arms over his head, took a deep breath, then stared out over the harbor.

"Excuse me, sir!" I spoke loudly.

He turned quickly, but didn't reply.

I approached slowly. "Nice evening, huh?" I noted the sarcasm in my voice.

He nodded. I could tell he was evaluating me – my badge – the gun. He pointed his hooked nose toward me and the wrinkles alongside his pale eyes deepened into a squint. Friend or foe? He wasn't sure how it would turn out. Neither was I.

I stopped three paces away. I was now certain this old man was not a threat. "Pretty late to be down this way, old timer," I said.

His sharp reply startled me. "You asking for a reason?"

"My name is Zachary, Edward Zachary. I grew up about six blocks away."

"You're a Locust Pointer?"

I laughed. "Yep. Went to Good Counsel, then to Saint Joe."

The breeze ruffled his stringy white hair and pushed several wild strands nearly straight up, and watched me for a long moment.

Then I hit him with the zinger. "I work for the Ecology Department."

His face gave nothing away. He must be a great poker player.

I was perturbed. "What's in your bucket, sir?"

Without looking down, he answered. "Crabs."

I considered this. "Crabs?" I asked skeptically. "I don't think so. They'd be in a frenzy to escape. Step aside, please."

I waited until he had backed up several paces, then I walked to the bucket and looked inside. The water was dark and quiet. I removed a flashlight from my shirt pocket. The sudden light caused the water to erupt with motion.

The bucket teemed with activity as small shapes jostled and jockeyed to escape the light. I leaned closer. There must have been thousands of creatures there. "Crabs?"

"Yep," he said proudly. "Chesapeake Blues. Just hatched."

I turned off the light and straightened. "Why?"

The old man regarded me. "Are you gonna arrest me?"

"Have you done anything wrong?" I asked.

"Just my moral duty."

There was a bench not far away. I motioned toward it. "Sit! We need to talk."

He looked out over the water, then hobbled toward the bench. Halfway there, he stopped and turned toward me. "I can't chat long, son. The tide is turning soon."

"And what does that mean?"

He pointed to the bucket. "Incoming tide – they'll get eaten in minutes. Outgoing – they might make the deeps."

He held out his hands for my inspection. "See these?"

Noting the scars, calouses, and discolorations, I nodded.

"Them's crabber hands." He pointed out along the Patapsco river toward the wide Bay. "All my life, I spent on those wooders. My father were a crabber – the best. He taught me ta set traps, and I was pretty dang good in my day." He thrust a hand closer to my face. "See 'em scars? From hauling lines, wire cuts, and crab bites." He laughed. "It were a good life. Out at dawn. Mostly alone - with my thoughts – and the crabs."

I nodded toward the bucket. "But, why this?"

His stare narrowed and he regarded me. "How many crabs you recon I caught - fifty year on the wooder?"

I shrugged.

"I figured it once – best I could." He looked towards his feet. "Too many!" Then his head snapped up defiantly. "Now I'm putting some back."

I could tell he wanted to say more. I waited.

"A friend gives me Blue Crab cows. I harvest the eggs and take care of 'em. When em're big enough, I put 'em back."

I started to talk, but he shook his head. "Every bucket has 'bout a thousand." He laughed again. "They ain't the prettiest things, I admit. I put in a couple buckets every night, so's eventually my debt's paid."

"But have you considered the impact of this?"

He didn't hesitate. "I been crabbin fifty years. Ain't that impact enough?"

The old fool didn't get it. I sighed deeply.

He continued. "I'm near seventy and been doing this for the past three summers. If the Good Lord gives me jus' ten more years, we'll be square."

I couldn't help laughing. It sounded harsh, but I didn't care. "You mean I've been waiting since sunset to confiscate a bucket of baby crabs…"

His look stopped me. Eyes watery with tears, he whispered. "Please! I owe it ta' the old Chesapeake. Don't 'ya see? What's a few more crabs matter?"

I felt an anger boiling inside me. "Matter! Thousands of extra crab hatchlings?"

He stared at me. I hit him the book answer – Glowacki's answer! "The mature crabs waiting below will feast on the hatchlings, sir. They won't scavenge like they should, so bacteria will breed out of control and algae will multiply. That's called 'Red Tide'. The Algae will consume oxygen from the water and fish will die. Dead fish will breed more bacteria. And Bingo! Ecological disaster and health hazard – all because you upset the eco-balance!"

The old man squinted at the bucket, then at me. His look told me he thought I was joking. "Extra crabs? Kill fish? Nope!"

"What? Why?"

He pointed to the harbor. "'Em are lazy crabs out there. Chasin babies is too hard. Besides, crab eggs is what fish love. More crabs in the wooder – more fish."

"How do you know that?" I yelled. "There's no science!"

"Science!" He spat the word, then tapped his head with a gnarly hand. "Crabs is what I know, sir!"

I stared at the bucket, then at the old man. Could he be right? Was the science really wrong? Was this old man a threat to anything? Did a few extra crabs even matter?

My anger suddenly fled. I had come searching for a criminal. Why? To justify my job? Validate my anger? Get even with that Glowacki woman? I hadn't expected to find a moral dilemma. Here was a citizen who wasn't polluting. He wasn't destroying anything. Yes, maybe he was violating a few regulations, but…while I had been enforcing silly rules, he was doing something positive - adding new life to the ecosystem. And, more important, he was gaining atonement for his sins - by the bucket.

I walked to the end of the pier and stared into the water. Across the harbor, the city slept. Camden Yards was dark. The Inner Harbor Complex was quiet. A tugboat glided southward on the smooth water. It was restful.

I stared into the bucket. The water had long since calmed, and the reflection from the lamp prevented me from seeing the life inside. I hefted the bucket, set it on the railing, then, smiling at the old man, I tipped it over.

The water splashed loudly into the dark harbor. For the briefest instant, the surface writhed with life, then it calmed - and I felt suddenly happier than I had in years.

I turned to the old man.

"I have a truck," I said. "Let's see how many buckets we can dump before morning."

YOSEMITE SAMUEL

The call came at around 0800 on a brisk Saturday morning. The Upper Falls Campground Manager reported that a hiker had not returned on schedule. Tent and gear still at Site #71. No other details. Despite my status as Head Ranger, I had the weekend duty for the Park Service, and it was my responsibility to investigate.

Ranger Dana Tomlin waited for me at the Campsite. Overhead, stratus clouds swirled west to east. Ominous clouds. We'd have snow by morning.

Dana Tomlin was what the other Rangers termed a "Hottie". Tall, well-proportioned, and Nordic. Despite the chill, she had removed her jacket and cap and her white-blonde hair hung half-way down her back. She was also a very good Ranger – one of the very best I had ever managed. Dedicated, professional, and interested in the public. I had promoted her over several more-senior Rangers. The Upper Falls Campground was hers – when she wasn't giving tours to school groups. The Park Service liked to show its best face to the public, and Dana Tomlin possessed the best face the Yosemite System had.

Dana held out a piece of paper toward me as I stepped from the staff car. Her breath emerged in misty puffs. "The camper is a Mister Samuel Haines, sir. An elderly gentleman. I would say in his seventies. He seemed very woods-wise. He was scheduled to be backpacking in the area yesterday and to return here to camp by evening. He didn't show. With the storm coming, I thought it best to investigate. I found this note when I looked through his things and I called you right away."

I examined the note. It had been typed on a computer.

"By the time you find this, you will know I didn't return to the Campground as planned. There's no need to search. I don't want to be found, and I will have hiked far into the backcountry by the time you read this. Call my son. I think he can explain it to you. Please don't put anyone in danger or go to any expense for me."

The note listed the name Sam Junior and a phone number. I pulled my cell phone from its holster adjacent to my revolver and punched the number.

"Sam Haines!" Came the reply.

"Mister Haines," I said. "My name is George Blomberg. I'm the Head Ranger at Yosemite Park. Is your father also named Samuel Haines?"

He paused. "Yes..."

"He's missing from the Yosemite Upper Falls Campground and a note he left says you might be able to tell us where he is."

Another pause. "Oh, dear! Listen, I live maybe two hours away. I'll be right there. You say the Upper Falls Campground?"

"Yes," I replied. "Are you familiar with it?"

"Good God, yeah! Dad and I camped and hiked from there every summer for 15 years. And he's been back many times by himself. He loves Upper Yosemite. Don't do anything until I get there, please!"

"We need to get a search organized, Mister Haines," I answered. "Your father is elderly and could be in trouble."

"Trust me," he replied. "Dad's not in trouble. He's a seasoned camper and he's in great shape. He knows those woods better than anyone – including your Rangers. He paused. "Besides, you won't find him."

"Why do you say that, Mister Haines?"

"Because, he doesn't want to be found, and I think I know why."

I considered the information. "Be here in two hours, Mister Haines. After that, we're going to start a search. It's the Park rules, and the first major snow storm of the season is due in here tonight."

"Wow! Dad has it all planned." The phone line went silent. I looked at Ranger Tomlin, then smiled. "His son is coming. He says the elder Mister Haines is an expert woodsman and may not want to be found."

I looked off into the tall pines that surrounded the campground. A stellar jay in a nearby tree squawked impatiently in my direction, vying for my attention. I watched the bird for several seconds while I made my decision.

Looking at Tomlin, I spoke quickly. "Call out the off-duty Rangers. Tell them we have a missing hiker. Ask them to assemble here in two hours and have their winter gear ready for a five-day hike into the backcountry. Also, alert Yosemite Headquarters to notify the local authorities. Tell them we don't need assistance at this point. Then have HQ get the chopper ready - on my authority. Tell them I'll be down there in 20 minutes and I'll ride the bird up this way."

Dana gave me a quizzical look.

I laughed. "I'm going along on the search, Ranger. I want to see if the Park Service and all its resources can rescue an old man who doesn't want to be found."

I started to turn for my car, but something about Dana's face stopped me. I frowned. "What's the matter Tomlin?"

"Sir, I'm tired of school groups and PR people. I want to see more of the backcountry. I want to come along."

I laughed. "Come along? Did you forget the Regs, Tomlin? Mister Haines is missing from your Campground. You're in charge of the operation. Put together a S&R Plan and be ready to discuss it when we assemble."

She smiled. "Thank you, sir!"

"Less thanks, more speed! You've got a lot to do, young lady. Get your gear."

"Yes, sir!" She hurried off toward her cabin, hair flying out behind her as she ran.

Sam Junior showed up precisely on time. He was a thin man, probably in his early thirties, handsome, athletic, with thick wavy dark hair and a thin matching mustache. He gawked at the group and the mountain of gear assembled around the site, then noticed the helicopter, blades spinning, at the far side of the campground.

He approached me.

"Chief Ranger Blomberg?" he asked. I nodded.

"I asked you to wait until I could explain," he said.

I waived an arm, indicating the Team assembled at the site. "We waited. Explain quickly, please. There's not much time."

He scanned the group. "I don't know everything, of course, but I can speculate."

"Well, get on with it." I replied.

He looked around the site, then pointed over my shoulder. "That's Dad's tent and gear. I recognize it."

Ranger Tomlin responded. "It looks like all he has with him are his backpack, a sleeping bag, water, and whatever food he was able to carry. He also left the foul weather gear and it's gonna get nasty up there real soon."

"He wouldn't have taken much food," he said. "He never over packed in all the years I've known him. And he won't need food."

"Explain yourself, Mister Haines. Just what's going on here?"

Haines looked at the loamy ground. "I think Dad's gone up there to die."

"Die, Mister Haines? You mean suicide?"

He shook his head. "Not really, but kinda."

I started to complain, but he raised a hand to cut me off. Then he walked to a picnic table and sat on the tabletop facing us. "It's difficult," he said, "but give me a minute and I can tell you why I think it's hopeless for you to risk your lives."

I surveyed the assembly. The Rangers eyed the gear. They knew we only had so many hours of light before we would have to make camp. They were anxious to get going. This was another adventure. They were cocky – not seasoned enough to understand risks. Tomlin, on the other hand, watched me closely. That was good. She wasn't reckless. She genuinely wanted to learn.

Haines continued. "Dad's what you would call a true woodsman. He grew up in Montana. He married Mom after University, and they moved to California to the Bay Area. He worked in the City, but he never lost his love of the forest. We would come with Mom to Yosemite a couple times every year to camp and hike – mostly spring and fall to avoid the crowds. I'll bet we hiked every National Park on the West Coast while I was growing. We even went winter camping in Alaska." He smiled at me. "I'll bet we've been here a hundred times together." He laughed. "I used to call him 'Yosemite Sam' when I was younger – it tickled him." He nodded toward the assembled Rangers. "Dad knows these woods - better than any of you."

Haines ignored the snorts of protest. He shook his head. "Mom died two years ago of heart failure. She and Dad had been married 50 years. They loved each other dearly – I've never seen a couple so dedicated. It devastated Dad when she died. At the funeral he took me aside. '*She promised me she wouldn't die first,*' he said. '*Who's gonna take care of us now, Sammy?*'"

Haines took a deep breath. "He hasn't been the same since. Can't sleep without pills. You never think of these things when you're young, but recently I realized that Mom was the one who kept the family going. Dad didn't know or care about the kitchen stuff, or about medications, or paying the bills. Late last Spring he called me and said he had left the gas burner on high all night and it scared him. He also said that Creditors had been calling, making threats. But he said the worst thing was that he had forgotten what Elise looked like, and that terrified him.

"He wouldn't come to live with me, so I stayed at the family house for two weeks last summer. I paid all the bills, and disconnected the gas at the stove, and we spent hours looking through the old albums. It was good for both of us. But more and more he would sit in the living room, staring at Mom's urn on the mantle. Before I left to get back to my own family, he pulled me aside, careful to whisper, he said, so that Mom wouldn't overhear. '*I'm going to become a doddering old fool, Sammy. I can feel myself slipping. I'm getting confused in the head. Pretty soon I won't be able to remember Elise or you even when I see the albums. It's no way to die, boy.*'"

Haines's eyes filled with tears. When he looked at the group, a drop tracked a slow path down his right cheek. "He's come here to die," he whispered.

"You can't know that!" one of the Rangers said loudly. "We're wasting time, and your Dad is out there."

I turned toward the speaker. "Enough! You're out of line!"

Haines answered. "I understand your enthusiasm, but I stopped by Dad's house on the way here." He paused. "Mom's urn is gone."

Dana gasped. "Oh, God! Poor man."

Haines sighed, then continued. "So is the medicine cabinet. I'll bet he's brought along enough sleeping pills to make sure he doesn't wake up."

The group was quiet now. Haines waited for several seconds before continuing. "Last year we spent two weeks in the back country. About a days' hike Northeast from here, we left the trail and descended into a secluded valley. It was a steep descent and I was afraid Dad would falter, but he's like an old mountain goat." Haines laughed suddenly. "He kept asking if I was okay."

Several of the Team laughed – Tomlin was loudest.

Haines continued. "It was a perfect day. Near the bottom, just at the tree line, we found some niches in the rock face – just big enough for a grown man to lie down, inside and out of the weather. Dad and I sat against the mountain face and had lunch. He remarked that the openings looked like the burial niches at the Catacombs. We agreed it was a gorgeous spot to rest, and look out over the valley below." He paused. "We both wished Mom could have been there to see it."

He nodded sharply. "I'll bet that's where he went. It's where he intends to die."

"Great!" A Ranger shouted. "I think I know the spot. Let's get started. We can take the helo and …"

Tomlin interrupted him "Not so fast, Sean!" she said.

I stared at Ranger Tomlin. "It's your Operation, Ranger. What do you think?"

"Too risky!"

I addressed her. "Explain yourself."

She nodded toward the scudding, darkening clouds. "Even if we started now, it's gonna be an hour of treacherous flying to get to the trailhead and then find a safe landing zone. By the time we hike to the point of descent, it would be too close to dark. The helo couldn't stay because it's going to start snowing tonight."

"So the helicopter comes back," a Ranger said. "We can get down to Mister Haines tomorrow morning and bring him up that afternoon."

"It won't work," Haines Junior interrupted, looking up at the sky. "The site's going to be under three feet of snow by morning and he'll be impossible to find." He chuckled. "Dad isn't quite senile yet. He timed this perfectly. He'll rock himself into one of the niches. Once the snows come, he'll be buried until spring. Spring thaws will bring new rockfall. Their resting place will probably be covered and safe - forever." He smiled. "He and Mom will have their spot overlooking the valley, and he won't grow old enough to be the forgetful old fool he feared."

I felt the pressure that had been building, release itself. I addressed Tomlin. "The S&R is cancelled?" I asked.

"Yes, sir! Too risky!"

"Well, the beer's on me!" the Ranger announced.

The Rangers collected their gear and dispersed. Haines Junior walked slowly to the campsite and began breaking down his father's camp.

Tomlin turned toward me. "I wish I could rename that valley after Elise for him." She frowned. "Does that make me a bad Ranger, sir?"

I laughed, and ignoring all regulations to the contrary, I patted her on the shoulder. "No, Ranger Tomlin. It makes you a good woman."

"Such a shame." She nodded. "I'll help Young Mister Haines pack." She started toward the campsite.

"Sammy?" A voice, thin and weak came from the wood's fifty yards away.

An old man stood at the edge of the forest. He stared at the young Haines. "You didn't come back like you promised, Sammy."

"Dad!" The younger Haines ran toward the old man.

"Mister Haines!" Dana yelled and ran as well.

When I joined the group they had clustered at a spot at the trees. Younger Haines had grabbed the elder in a bear hug and spun him around. The old man faced me. I could read confusion on his features. He seemed disoriented. "Where did you go?" he asked. "Why are you packing?"

"We thought you were lost," Dana said.

"Lost? Is that what you told them, Sammy."

The younger Haines stepped backward and spread his arms. "No dad. Remember. I was in San Francisco. You got lost. I came to help."

Elder Haines remained silent for several moments. "Your plan didn't work, Sammy. I'm still alive."

Young Haines frowned, then approached the old man. "Dad, Dad. What are you talking about? Let's go home."

Dana eyed me warily. I nodded. She slipped away.

"Where's she going?" Sammy Haines asked.

"To report Mr. Haines as safe. Standard procedure. Let's sit down at that picnic table," I suggested. "So we can wrap this up. We need to file a report."

"Okay, but let's hurry. I need to get dad to a Doctor."

Dana joined us. Once seated, I turned to the elder Haines. "What happened, Mister Haines?"

As he replied, the old man's eyes never left his son.

"I came to camp like I usually do this time of year. Sammy said he was too busy to come."

"Right! Like I said. I stayed behind," Sammy interrupted.

"But he showed up unexpectedly yesterday as I was leaving."

"You're imagining all this. Did you take your pills, Dad?"

"We hiked together on the trail for five, maybe six hours," the elder Haines continued. "South along the ridge."

Dana spoke. "You said he would go north, Mister Haines."

The old man continued. "Then we turned east on an old logging trail and stopped to eat after another couple hours."

Young Haines looked at me. He smiled and shrugged. "See what I deal with? None of this happened."

Samuel Haines continued. "I think he tried to drug me. Told me he had some new medication I was supposed to take."

"Dad! How can you say that?"

"He got me to sign some legal papers, then took off last evening when he thought I was asleep. I was suspicious and only pretended to take the pills."

Sammy Haines laughed. "Dad. You can't expect them to believe that I hiked ten miles in the dark over rough trails, drove back to San Francisco, and got there in time to get their distress call this morning? I'd have to be superman."

"More likely desperate," the old man announced.

"Dad! Stop please. I need to get you home."

Samuel Haines stood, then came around behind me. "What a son! He wanted to kill me and steal my money."

In the distance the sounds of sirens coming nearer. That would be the Park Police. Sam Junior looked at Dana and me and shifted uncomfortably. I quietly unholstered my weapon and indicated to Dana that she should do the same. I put the gun carefully on the bench next to me – out of sight.

Samuel Hanes leaned across the table and stared hard at Sammy. "Wait a minute! You're not my son. Who are you?"

The way he said it alerted me. Something wasn't right. I reached down for the weapon. It was gone.

"What did you do with my son?" Samuel Hanes shouted. "Impostor!" His hand came up quickly and he fired. Across the table Sammy Haines yelled. "Dad!" a single time, then fell backward off his seat. Dana screamed.

I jumped to my feet – only to face my own weapon – pointed between my eyes. "Dana!" I said as calmly as I could. "Call for an ambulance, then tend to young Haines."

Samuel Haines stared at me. "He was an impostor."

"Who?"

He nodded across the table. "Him! He said he was my son."

"He is your son, Mister Haines."

He shook his head. "Did I have a son?" He looked down. "It gets so confusing sometimes."

I slowly reached out and pushed the revolver aside, then took it from him. "How does it look over there, Dana?" I asked.

"He's going to survive, I think," Dana replied. "I called for an ambulance."

I put a hand on the old man's shoulder. "Sit down, Mister Haines. Let's wait for the Police to straighten this out."

"Why do you suppose he did it?" he asked me suddenly.

"Did what?"

"Tried to poison me like that." He reached into his shirt pocket. "I kept the pills he gave me. Elise will bear me out. Where is she?" He handed me four small white tablets.

The Park Police and ambulance arrived together. Dana and I waited to one side while they did their work. "Can I speak to you?" she whispered.

"Of course."

She turned away from the activity and I turned as well. From a pocket of her vest she removed a leather pouch. It had been punctured by the bullet. "Look at this," she said. "I took this out of the young Haines' jacket pocket when I was examining the wound. It's only leather, but I think it helped slow the bullet. It may have saved his life."

I smiled. "Amazing luck," I said.

"That's not all," she continued. She opened the pouch. Inside was a document, a hole torn neatly through the middle. "I only just now looked at it," she added.

I read the first page. "A Voluntary Commitment Document," I whispered.

"Signed yesterday by the younger Haines and an attorney."

I rifled through some more pages. "There is also an Agreement to transfer assets to the younger Haines." I whistled. "Worth quite a lot of money."

"Look at the final page," she said. "See the date?"

The final page contained the signatures of both the younger and elder Haines - dated yesterday. "So Sammy did come up here," I said. "The old man was right."

I looked closer. "But the joke is still on Sammy Hanes."

"Why's that?" she asked.

I showed her the final page again. "Because he didn't take time to look at the signature."

She stared. "Oh, my God. Yosemite Samuel!"

PROMISES

    I hate public transportation. Always have. Especially here in Baltimore. Late busses. Jostling crowds. Poor customer service. Rude passengers. Wierdos of every stripe. My list of complaints goes on. And, God help me, I work for the MTA! I'm what they call an inspector. I ride the bus lines all day - watching, noting, reporting. Nothing ever changes, but they pay me, and I'm two years from retirement.

    I don't usually work on Sundays, but, with Nancy out of town I got restless the past three weekends, and so I've taken to riding the busses – mostly the longer runs. Sometimes I sit up front and chat with the drivers. Other times I nestle into the farthest rear seat and observe the passengers. What a book I could write someday about the things I've seen.

    I sold the house in Woodlawn after it got too depressing to go home. Now I live in a two-room walk-up in Federal Hill – a block from where I was born 62 years ago.

    Anyway, I decided today was a rear seat day, and I climbed on board the Number 2 at the corner of Light Street and Fort Avenue around noon – it was twenty minutes late of course - and I got off at the Civic Center to catch the Number 23 to Glen Burnie. On weekdays it was a two-hour trip. Today the driver should make it in 90 minutes.

    There weren't many passengers, and none were particularly interesting, so I began reminiscing – my usual daydream – what the hell was I going to do with retirement coming and all our kids scattered to the four winds?

    The bus had just entered Brooklyn when the old man got on. He was probably seventy-five, skinny, with thick hair gone white, and a somber look that interested me immediately. Not so much because I thought he was going to be trouble, but because he had the classic look of an interesting passenger. I perked up.

    Coins tinkling loudly, he paid his fare and started down the aisle. I inspected him. He looked uncomfortable in the dark suit that hung too loosely around his shoulders. And the collar of his starched white shirt was two or three sizes too large. And his tie was hopelessly out of date. More intriguing was the bouquet of flowers that he cradled across an arm.

I don't often chat with the passengers, but I had to know what this man was doing, so when he chose a seat midway down the right side of the bus, I moved to a place behind him. He had sidled over to the window, but didn't look outside. Instead he gazed ahead toward the front of the bus, but it was clear to me he wasn't watching anything in particular.

Before speaking, I took note of his grizzled features, the hard line of his jaw, the thin lips, and even the thick clumps of white hair in his ears. Here was a man with a story.

"Excuse me sir," I said tentatively.

At first I thought he hadn't heard me, and I began to speak again, when he shook his head, then turned in my direction.

"Huh?"

I smiled. "Excuse me," I said. "I couldn't help but notice how well dressed you are…" I nodded toward the bouquet. "And the flowers. I don't mean to pry, but where are you headed?"

He stared at me for a moment, confused, then a look of recognition came over him. He nodded. "Holy Cross," he said, then continued his blank forward stare.

Now I understood the whole thing. He was going to Holy Cross Cemetery. Just on the other side of Brooklyn where Ritchie Highway meets the Beltway.

"Visiting a loved one?" I asked.

Again he hesitated. "Buried my wife last week."

My own emotions flooded over me. "I am so sorry. How long were you married?"

He turned most of the way around. "More'n fifty years."

"Wow! Long time," I commented. "Going to visit the grave already?" Then I realized that I didn't know the graveside visitation protocol. Nancy and I had requested that we be cremated when our time came and that our ashes scattered near our summer home in Ocean City. So there were to be no cemetery visits for either of us.

He stared. "I couldn't do it all proper at the funeral. So's I figured I'd come back when it'd be private like."

"I see," I answered. I felt an admiration for the man and pictured him, week after week, standing by the grave, silent, reverent, waiting for his own passing.

"Fifty years is a long time," I said. It must have been quite a marriage."

He squinched up his eyes and paused. He seemed to be lost in thought.

After a moment he spoke again. "We raised ten kids. Most of 'em turned out all right, I guess."

"My Nancy and me, are married forty-two years," I replied.

He looked down at his lap. I thought I saw him grimace. "Ruth got sick. Lots of pain at the end."

I spoke quickly. "But the two of you must have really loved each other, huh?"

"They was good years and bad years," he replied.

"Oh, us too!" I said. "We had three kids. You know how hard raising kids can be. All of mine are grown and have their own families. One lives in California, another in Texas, the third in Tidewater Virginia."

He nodded. "Mine're all over the place, too."

I pointed to the flowers. "Nice touch," I said.

He shrugged.

"Did your entire family come back for the funeral?" I asked.

He nodded. "Most of 'em"

"Great!"

"Listen," I said. "I hope I'm not bothering you."

He shrugged. "Guess not."

I moved the seat beside him and held out a hand as I sat. "My name is Roland Merkowsko. I live down in Locust Point."

He shook my hand loosely. "Bernie," he said. "Bernie McClanahan."

"Well, Mr. McClanahan. I admire your devotion."

"You do?"

"Certainly," I replied. "Visiting the grave not a week after she's buried. That takes a lot of gumption, if you ask me."

"I didn't wanna wait too long afore I did what I promised."

I patted his arm. "I understand. I really do."

He shook his head. "I don't think ya do."

"No, no," I protested. "Nancy and I are like a team. We know what the other is thinking. We are together nearly every moment." I paused. "It's like magic sometimes."

"She drank too much," he blurted.

I smiled. "We all have our vices, Mr. McClanahan."

He chuckled. "God. She'd get rip-roaring drunk sometimes. Don't know why. Me. I hardly touch the stuff."

"But you weathered that challenge," I offered.

"She had a temper too. Awful bad."

I nodded. "I can understand that. Ten kids and all. It must have driven her crazy sometimes."

"Sure drove me crazy." He answered. "But I promised."

"You stayed married fifty years, Mr. McClanahan. That's remarkable."

"She wouldn't hear of divorce," he answered. "We're Catholic, ya know."

"A name like McClanahan, what else would you be?" I replied.

"Yep," he said. "I put up with an awful lot over the years."

I nodded vigorously. "It's the sign of a strong marriage."

He stared at me for a long time. "Say," he asked. "Since you admire me so much, would ya do me a big favor?"

"If I can," I answered.

"Good! Come with me ta' Holy Cross." He fumbled in a side pocket of his suit and pulled out a disposable camera. "I want ta have a pichur 'a me at the grave."

"You want me to take a photo?"

"Yeah!" he replied. "That'd be great! I promised, 'ya see."

I didn't hesitate. "Of course. I was riding the bus for fun. I'd be happy to go with you."

He wrinkled his nose. "Ya ride this thing for fun?"

I laughed. "Yes. Sort of. It relaxes me."

He nodded, but he clearly didn't understand.

The Cemetery was another two miles down the road near the top of a grassy hill. The bus stop was at the entrance. White washed concrete walls marked the entry. The walls were cracked, and grass flagged through fissures in the narrow asphalt drive. Above the entry drive, a wrought iron sign identified the place as *Holy Cross Cemetery*. A smaller, hand-painted sign proclaimed that visitors must check in at the office. There didn't seem to be many visitors.

Once off the bus, Mr. McClanahan held the flowers erect, and started up the road. "It's time ta keep my promises, he announced. "Grave 2371. It's on the west side."

I followed him through the gates and into another world. Despite the traffic roaring past on Ritchie Highway, Holy Cross Cemetery was strangely quiet. I had never been a fan of cemeteries and probably hadn't been to more than three in my whole life. The whole maudlin grief routine was what prompted Nancy and I toward cremation.

McClanahan led me up a small rise and around a traffic circle. In the center of the circle was a white marble pedestal more than ten feet in diameter, atop which stood a carved angel brandishing a sword toward heaven.

McClanahan looked back at me. "Michael," he said.

"What?"

"The archangel. He protects souls on the way ta' heaven."

The small of grass was overwhelming. I could imagine a green fog of chlorophyll surrounding us. We continued forward to where the site leveled off. Around us was a curious mix of flat markers, tombstones, mausoleums, and elaborate memorials. It was hard to imagine all those dead people lying so near to each other – strangers in a far stranger land.

"This way," McClanahan announced, and he turned right along a small asphalt roadway, hardly big enough for a single car.

I followed him, keenly award of being surrounded by so much death. Would it have been better to have graves and lie side-by-side for eternity?

Mr. McClanahan led me fifty yards down the lane, then stopped. There was a spot, ten or so paces out into the flat grass, where the earth had been newly turned and covered with fresh sod. He stared at the spot. "It's her'n," he announced, then he handed me the camera. "Take pichurs when I say."

Holding the flowers against his chest, he walked very slowly out onto the field. His shoulders slumped as he moved forward. He looked tired. I felt sympathy for the old fellow - putting himself through such an ordeal without the benefit of family support.

I spoke soft words. "Are you okay, Mr. McClanahan?"

He nodded, barely. "I made a promise. Start tak'in 'em pichurs," he said.

He approached the grave, then stopped. Carefully, he leaned over and put the flowers in the center of the slight mound that marked the site.

I snapped a photo.

Then he stepped forward and put a foot atop the dirt. Then the second foot. He now stood on the center of the grave.

I snapped another photo.

"I promised ya, Ruthie. I'm here ta keep ma promise."

He lifted his right foot and stomped it down hard on the sod. Then he lifted his left and did the same thing. He repeated the steps, gaining speed and momentum, and hopping about nearly as spryly as a young man. It took me a full thirty seconds of observing to realize he was dancing an Irish jig.

I took another photo.

Then he began to sing.

"Ding dong the bitch is dead
Which old bitch? The wicked bitch.
Ding dong the wicked bitch is dead!"

I felt an overwhelming sense of shock, and brought the camera down until it rested at my side.

His dancing had brought him around until he faced me.

"Keep takin pichurs!" he yelled.

"But Mr. McClanahan…"

"Pichurs!" he yelled again. "Ah'm keeping my promise!" He was smiling.

I raised a camera and snapped another photo.

It took more than five minutes for him to expend his energy. When he finished, he trudged to where I stood. I handed him the camera. "I used up the whole roll," I said.

He smiled. "Good man."

"Why, Mr. McClanahan?"

He nodded. "'Cause she was the Queen of the Harpies. She made my life miserable for fifty years. She tormented the children. She never had a kind word to say to anyone."

He paused, and his tired eyes searched my face. "I promised her that if she died afore me, I'd dance on her grave for all the pain she caused. It was one promise ah'm glad ta keep."

"But you stayed married for fifty years?" I offered. "There must have been something redeeming in all that time."

He smiled. "Nope!" Then he turned his back and headed toward the main avenue. "I've spent 'nough time rubbin it in, I guess. Now it's my turn to live." He laughed. "Think I can do another thirty years?" he joked.

I stared at the grave for a moment as he walked away. I noted the trampling and the uneven sod – and the flowers strewn across the fresh sod.

"But, Mr. McClanahan," I half shouted. "The flowers. Why the flowers?"

He didn't turn back. "She was allergic," he announced and continued down the path.

THE END OF THINGS

"Damn it!" Clayton Wilson shouted - his harsh Tennessee accent grating every word. "I say we sell!" As we paced the picket fencing, I noted his face reddening and the tendons in his bull neck stretching like taut cords. "It's our best chance!"

Elaine stopped walking, and when she shook her head, auburn hair shimmered in the sunlight. She was so damn beautiful, I had to smile. "Now, Clayton!" she said patiently in a soft voice. "Let's don't be too hasty about this."

"Hasty?" Clayton asked. "There's more'n a million dollars at stake, Elaine."

Marshall, the younger brother, waved his arms for emphasis. He was a head shorter that Clayton and darker haired. "I talked with Mister Bowdon this morning, Elaine, and the deal is ready. All we have to do is sign!"

"Well," Elaine said loudly, "you should have consulted me – and daddy!"

"You know right well," Clayton scoffed, "that daddy wouldn't approve. But it ain't for him to say no more."

Elaine's voice raised another octave and she spread her arms. "He's not dead yet, Clayton! This is still his farm. He has every right to know."

"Sorry, Elaine," Marshall said, "We have Power of Attorney."

I looked down the fence toward the hill and remembered a time - ten years past.

"Taste that air?" The old man had asked. His nostrils flared to catch the slight breeze. He smiled, and the skin beside his pale blue eyes crinkled like raisins.

I sniffed, smelled nothing unusual, then shrugged.

He chuckled, as if to brand me as the city slicker that I am, and with a hand tanned to nearly the color of the loamy soil, the old man plucked a sprig of dried grass. Sniffing the breeze tentatively, he tossed it into the air. It fluttered to the ground. He nodded once sharply, then looked at me. "Yep! Air's wet and wind's from the west. Rain by morning."

I scanned the sky for any sign of cloud and found none.

He hadn't waited for my approval. In quick easy steps, he moved under the trees.

Although I considered myself athletic, I had to hurry to catch up, and not get dust on my loafers.

He spoke over his shoulder. "My great granddaddy planted these pear trees in eighteen sixty two – right after he come home to Tennessee from the war." He turned toward me, then swept his arm in a wide panorama. "'Cept for this here hill, all the family land used to be farmed, but this spot was too rocky and weren't good for much. The old families tried beans and alfalfa, but never could make 'em grow right."

He turned away. "Follow me!" He started up the hill.

"This here's what we call '*Major's Hill*' after the first Wilson to settle in these parts. Major Albemarle Wilson – one of Washington's top aides. Fought beside the good General at Trenton, and on the road to Virginia."

He stopped suddenly, startling me. "Bet ya didn't know Elaine was related to a war hero, now did ya, Bradley?"

"Ah…no!"

He continued his effortless strides up the hill, and I huffed after him. It had been cool in the shadow of the trees, but, when we emerged in sunlight, I began to sweat.

Above the trees, the crest of the short hill was bare of all but knee-high grass that waved in the steady breeze. Except for the Chahaugua River, meandering in lazy loops to the west, and the dark swath of Interstate Highway that cleaved the valley relentlessly from end to end, an irregular vista of patchwork farms and woods stretched on every side to far off rolling hills, blue in the late afternoon light. "The Smokies!" he pronounced.

He pointed a finger toward the road. "Wilsons owned all the property from the River to the far hills. Ceded by the First Continental Congress. Each generation split the land among its children." He indicated the land closer by. "When I die, Clayton will get a farm house and a hundred acres west along the highway. Marshall will have himself a ninety-acre farm next to him. And Elaine will get the orchard, and the fifty acres that stretch from their farms to the river." He chuckled. "Don't tell 'ma boys, but she's getting the best of it 'cause she gets the orchard – it was her mama's pride and joy."

Squinting into the setting sun, he considered the land. "More'n two hundred years, Wilsons have been farming this land. It's a right long time, and our roots are deep in this here Tennessee soil."

Then he turned to me. "I thought you had a right to know the plan since my daughter has her mind set to marrying you."

"I guess she does, doesn't she?" I laughed.

It rained a gully washer that evening before bed.

As Clayton's voice rose to a near shout, his words carried over the empty fields toward the farmhouse a half-mile distant. Delvin Wilson's farmhouse. I tried to picture the proud old man, bed-ridden and growing weaker by the minute.

"I am sick to death of farming, Elaine!" Clayton roared. "Of working dusk to dawn for next to nothing. And Paula and the kids want their daddy around."

"This is the best chance we have," Marshall added. His eyes shone with a pleading quality that embarrassed me.

"I'm not convinced!" Elaine said.

"Why the hell not?" Clayton exploded. "You ain't coming back here to Tennessee after papa's dead. Give up your Executive position? You gonna live in the old house, Elaine? You gonna tend the orchard? You gonna harvest and sell the pears?"

Elaine's shoulders slumped, and she stared at the dirt. "I don't know, Clayton. It was mama's orchard. Those pears are the best in the State."

Clayton laughed. "Sure! Pack up your children out of the fancy private schools and come back to the farm. Have Bradley here quit his high and mighty job. And, in case you ain't looked in a mirror for the last twenty years, you are about as old and run down as I am. You ain't got the energy to do that back-breaking work, Elaine - and Bradley here sure can't."

While part of me resented Clayton's implication, another part recognized the truth. I decided to keep my mouth shut.

"But it's the family farm!" she replied, her voice weak and haunted.

I looked away again.

"I want to show you something else," Delvin had said. "Follow me!"

He led me across the crest of the hill to the east side. Halfway down the slope, two poplar trees shaded a small neatly-tended yard fenced with white pickets. As we approached, his pace slowed.

Inside the fence were rows of graves, each marked with a small marble headstone. He turned to me. "They planted the first Wilsons on the east side so they could face the homes and families they left behind." He nodded. "This here was Injin Territory when they settled. It were a hard life."

He indicated the far side of the plot, where the stones were weathered. "The Major's wife died of fever the second year. His oldest son was killed by a wild redskin. The Major lived on another twenty years and is buried a'tween the two of 'em."

He paused, and I could see tears well up in his eyes as he nodded to a closer spot. "Margaret is buried right there, just inside the gate. It's where she wanted. So she could see family what comes and goes and greet them that stays, personal like."

He wiped at his eyes. "Soon enough I'll be next to her, I reckon."

He turned toward me. "I guess after two hundred years, you and the land become one." He sighed. "It'll be good to go home, Bradley."

Elaine stared from one brother to the other, then looked at me. "What do you think, Brad?"

Clayton's face became even redder as he glared at me. "He's got no say in this, Elaine!" He shouted

He had once been handsome – a local ladies man, as Elaine put it. But his stocky frame had turned soft and pudgy, and his once-blond hair had dulled to gray. Soon it would be silver like his father's.

"I agree with Clayton!" I answered. "It's not my decision."

"See!" Clayton said.

"I don't care what you two ninnies think!" Elaine pronounced. "I want to hear my husband's ideas." She stared at me.

"I shouldn't get involved in family squabbles," I offered lamely.

"You are involved," Elaine said. "I want to know what you think."

"I don't know what to think, Elaine."

Delvin Wilson had indicated the nearest tree. "We done harvested all the pears, but they's few left. See 'em? Green but turnin yella fast. Just as sweet as can be. Don't know why, but everyone says they's the best in all the South. I caint rightly say that's a fact, but I do believe it to be so."

I looked down the long row of trees, then over at the identical rows that stretched for more than a quarter mile. "You harvested all these yourself?"

He laughed. "'Course not! Every year the Cruz family comes up from Mexico and it's mostly their younguns that do the work. Misses Cruz is Margarita – funny thing - same name as my Margaret. For two weeks every year those two used to cook up a storm, laughing and telling secrets. Don't know how they communicated – but women somehow do." He paused. "Margarita cried for days when she heard 'about the passin."

He stared away and his eyes welled up again. "Good people, the Cruzes."

"You gotta get the pears when they's just ready. Right when you can bite and taste the beginnins of sugar. And you caint throw 'em in a bin. They've gotta be boxed on the spot – pointy ends up. Each one kept apart with tissue paper to save the freshness."

He found a low-growing pear that had somehow been missed, and snapped it from its branch. "Here! Taste of it!"

I turned the pear in my hands and brought it to my nose. The skin, just the slightest bit soft, smelled tangy. I bit, first a small piece, then a larger chuck. The flesh pulled away with the barest snap, and my mouth filled with juices that made my jaws ache for more.

Wiping my mouth with the back of a hand, I smiled. "Delicious!" It was hardly an apt appraisal, but it would have to do.

Delvin waited, smiling, as I finished the pear, then he nodded and his voice turned serious. "The harvest lasts no more than two weeks, but all the machinery and supplies have to be here ahead of time." He pointed a finger at me for emphasis. "Especially the boxes! 'Ya caint forget the boxes."

Clayton was calm. "Let me explain this again, Elaine. You remember old Mister Bowden - used to own the Ford Dealership in Miller's Crossing? Well his son is a developer. Harlan Junior has some Yankee money interested in this land for a resort. Condominiums, a spa, golf courses, boating on the river. He'll pay the three of us one million, two hundred thousand for the land. That's four hundred thousand each!"

"I can do the math, Clayton!" Elaine snapped. "But this is family land! It's not rental property or investment acreage. Our ancestors have been here for more than two hundred years. If we sell, the Albemarle Wilsons will cease to exist in Tennessee."

"That just ain't true!" Clayton exploded. "Marshall and I will still live here! It's y'all who's run away."

Elaine pointed a finger at Clayton. "That's not what I meant, and you know it! It's not the name. It's the land! Daddy loves the land, and we'll be giving it away."

"Selling it, Elaine. For a million dollars! There's a big difference."

"Besides," Marshall added. "What else can we do?"

Elaine turned to me again. "Help me, Brad. What can I do?"

My mind raced furiously.

"Y'all have to sell!" Clayton shouted.

"I can't!" she said staring at me.

"We caint farm this land for profit, Elaine," Marshall added.

Elaine's pleading look and Marshall's words touched some chord. My brain began to whirl. I watched Elaine - her features reminded me of her proud father. She might live in New York, but she was the land too!

"Help me, Bradley!"

I couldn't believe the next words that rushed from my mouth. "You don't have sell, Marshall! I promise you'll have your money, Clayton – and then some!"

The brothers looked at me skeptically.

The graves were neatly tended as always. Elaine would have a fit if they weren't.

"There they are!" she said softly.

Two marble stones rested beside each other. Delvin and Margaret Wilson. Comfortable. At home.

Elaine squeezed my arm. "You, sir, are a genius!"

I shook my head. "Not really! The solution was so simple, but the family was too close to it to see. We cut out all the middlemen and did it ourselves – our way."

"Clayton is in his glory," she whispered. "Can you imagine? President for Life of the Wilson Heritage Golf and Country Club. All the country music stars are paying a fortune to belong."

"And," I added. "Marshall is perfect as the Albemarle Acres condominium manager."

She smiled. "But keeping the orchard was the most brilliant thing!"

"Hey!" I said. "Those are great pears! A little advertising. A production facility. It was a sure thing."

"It's wonderful, Brad! Wilson Orchards. Profitable in its first year."

"How could it fail with you in charge?"

She laughed.

"But you know what's best?" I added.

She smiled at me.

"When the Cruz family comes to harvest," I continued. "Hearing you and Missus Cruz in the kitchen. Laughing and telling secrets. I know what Delvin meant. It's so comforting."

She shook her lovely head. "No, Brad. Not comforting. It's home."

Made in the USA
Columbia, SC
13 February 2025